Willliam Francis Collier

History of Greece

Anatiposi

Willliam Francis Collier

History of Greece

Reprint of the original, first published in 1872.

1st Edition 2023 | ISBN: 978-3-38212-873-9

Anatiposi Verlag is an imprint of Outlook Verlagsgesellschaft mbH.

Verlag (Publisher): Outlook Verlag GmbH, Zeilweg 44, 60439 Frankfurt, Deutschland
Vertretungsberechtigt (Authorized to represent): E. Roepke, Zeilweg 44, 60439 Frankfurt, Deutschland
Druck (Print): Books on Demand GmbH, In de Tarpen 42, 22848 Norderstedt, Deutschland

Nelson's School Series.

HISTORY OF GREECE.

BY

WILLIAM FRANCIS COLLIER, LL.D.,
TRINITY COLLEGE, DUBLIN;
Author of "School History of the British Empire," "English History for Junior Classes," "The Great Events of History," "History of English Literature," &c.

LONDON:
T. NELSON AND SONS, PATERNOSTER ROW
EDINBURGH; AND NEW YORK.
MDCCCLXXII.

DR. COLLIER'S HISTORIES OF GREECE AND ROME.

(Each to be had separately.)

NOTE.

THESE volumes aim at giving a clear outline of the chief events in Grecian and Roman History.

The personal or biographical element, upon which so much of the living interest of History mainly depends, has been kept prominently in view throughout.

The same plan has been followed as that adopted in the author's "Great Events of History;" and among other features of similarity to that work, these volumes contain Lists, which will enable a pupil to become acquainted with the leading names in Greek and Roman Literature.

June, 1866.

CONTENTS.

FIRST PERIOD.

SECOND PERIOD.

THIRD PERIOD.

HISTORY OF GREECE.

FIRST PERIOD.

CHAPTER I.

LEGENDS OF THE HEROIC AGE.

Early Races. | The Golden Fleece.
Hercules. | Trojan War.
Theseus.

GREECE, the most easterly and most broken of the three peninsulas in which Southern Europe terminates, was in ancient times the abode of a nation, which shone in arms, in arts, in literature, and in philosophy with a lustre that surpassed the glory of all surrounding lands.

It is impossible in sketches like these to give any account of the speculations of modern scholars regarding the various original races, which occupied the soil of this favoured territory, and laid the groundwork of the several states that made up ancient Greece. Let it suffice to say that there existed in the land, previous to the spread of the Hellenes, a population composed of various tribes or races, among which the most powerful were the Pelasgians; and then, after the lapse of time, there came from a little spot in Southern Thessaly, at the base of Mount Othrys, a race more powerful than all—probably a Pelasgian branch filled with the purest blood of the national stem—who under the name of Hellenes overspread the country, and stamped their name upon it in the title *Hellas*. This title afterwards gave place to the Roman name *Greece*. Of the Hellenes there were four sections, named from certain chiefs or heroes—Æolians, Achæans, Dorians, and Ionians.

About the arrival in Greece of certain emigrants from foreign lands, there are legends which may be noticed here, although it must be remembered that they are stories resting upon no solid foundation. Such settlements are ascribed to a time previous to the dominion of the Hellenes. Four are chiefly mentioned.

It is said that Danaus, coming from Egypt, founded Larissa, afterwards the citadel of Argos; that Cecrops, also an Egyptian, founded Athens, which took its name in honour of Athene or Minerva; that Cadmus not only led a Phœnician colony into Bœotia and founded Cadmea, which grew into Thebes, but also introduced the knowledge of the alphabet into Greece; and that Pelops was a rich chieftain from Asia, who established a new dynasty in Argos, and gave his name to the leaf-shaped peninsula.

After these things came a time called the Heroic Age, lasting about two hundred years, and rich in such tales of adventure as the romancers and minstrels of a primitive age love to recount and to embellish. There is much poetic beauty in these legends, not unmingled with a substratum of history; but it is impossible either to accept them as entirely true, or to discover how much of any tale is authentic. I now proceed to narrate the four principal legends of the Heroic Age, in the form in which they have descended to us.

I. *The Legend of Hercules.*—Hercules (in Greek Heracles) was a demi-god, the son of Zeus (Jupiter) and Alcmene of Thebes in Bœotia. His stepfather was Amphitryon. As he and his baby-brother were lying in the cradle, two snakes, sent by the jealous Hera (Juno), glided in, and would have killed the children, had not the infant hero grasped them in his tiny hands and choked them to death. His education resembled that of a mediæval knight; for he was instructed in driving, wrestling, archery, and music. Having killed his music-master with a lyre, he was banished by his stepfather, and went to herd cattle on the slopes of Cithaeron, where he killed a lion, whose skin he wore. When he grew to manhood, he received arms from the gods, and by order of Eurystheus, King of Argos, under whose dominion he had fallen, proceeded to accomplish the twelve Labours, which are so often alluded to in literature that I must give a brief notice of them.

1. Having gone to fight the Nemean lion, he used his brazen club and arrows in vain; nor could he vanquish the monster, until he stopped up one mouth of its den, and entering the other, strangled it with his naked hands.

2. He also slew the Lernean hydra, a nine-headed water-snake. As fast as he cut off the heads, others grew up, until he thought of making his servant burn the stumps. The middle head, which was immortal, he buried under a rock. He then dipped his arrows in the bile of the snake to poison their points.

3. After a year's chase he caught a stag of Arcadia with golden antlers and brazen feet.

4. Hunting the Erymanthian boar in the snow, he caught it in a net, and carried it to Mycenae.

5. By turning two rivers from their channels he cleansed the stables of Augeas, King of Elis, where innumerable herds of cattle were constantly kept.

6. Rousing with the noise of a metallic rattle the brazen-clawed birds of Stymphalus, which used their feathers as hurtful darts, he shot them with his arrows as they flew.

7. He seized and carried off upon his shoulders a bull belonging to Minos of Crete.

8. He captured the mares of Thracian Diomedes, who fed them on human flesh. They ate one of his friends, in whose charge he had left them; but he brought them triumphantly to their destination.

9. He obtained the girdle of the Amazonian Queen Hippolyte.

10. He undertook a long journey to seize the red oxen of the three-bodied monster Geryon, who lived at the setting sun, and accomplished his purpose, after having slain a giant and a two-headed dog.

11. He took some of the golden fruit of the Hesperides in spite of the sleepless dragon that guarded it.

12. Having descended into the infernal regions, he dragged the watch-dog Cerberus into the upper light for a time.

Wherever the blinking and sneezing brute let its spittle fall, plants of deadly aconite grew up.

Having killed a boy by accident at a feast, Hercules went into banishment with his wife. At a certain river he employed the Centaur Nessus to carry her across the flood; but this creature offered her so gross an insult that Hercules, standing on the other side, cleft his heart with an arrow. The dying Centaur bade Dejaneira keep his blood, which would restore to her the wandering affection of her lord. She did so; and on one occasion, when Hercules after a long absence from home sent to her for a white garment, that he might offer sacrifice, she dipped the dress in the blood and sent it to him. He had scarcely donned it, when racking pain shot through every limb. He tried to tear off the robe; but the flesh, to which it had stuck, came off in pieces. In his rage and anguish he hurled the messenger, who had brought the dress, into the sea; and then, ascending Mount Œta, built a pile of wood, on which he lay down. A passing shepherd lit the pyre, and the hero ascended to Olympus in clouds and thunder.

II. *The Legend of Theseus.*—Very similar to the story of Hercules is that of Theseus the hero of Attica. Ægeus, King of Athens, was his father; and, when he had reached manhood, his mother, Æthra of Troezen, showed him a large rock, under which he found the sword and sandals of his sire. Equipped with these, he made his way to Attica, not by the usual sea route, but by land, in spite of the monsters and robbers that beset the way. When he came to Athens, he found the sorceress Medea living with his father: she tried to poison the illustrious youth; but the sight of the well-known sword caused Ægeus to recognize and welcome his son.

The grand exploit of Theseus was the slaughter of the Minotaur, a monster, half-man half-bull, which was kept in a labyrinth in Crete, and fed every nine years with the flower of the Athenian youth. He achieved this exploit by the aid of Ariadne, the daughter of Minos, who fell in love with him, and aided him to escape from the windings of the maze. He ill repaid her devotion, for he deserted her at Naxos, and left her weeping on the shore. It had been agreed between his father and him, that, if the attempt to slay the Minotaur proved successful, the returning ship should hoist *white* sails. Theseus forgot to do so; and old Ægeus, judging the worst from the dark shrouds of the approaching ship, threw himself from a rock. Theseus then reigned in his stead.

Many and varied were his adventures and exploits as King. He fought with the Amazons. He carried off the famous Helen, when a mere child, from Sparta. And he even descended to the infernal regions for the purpose of robbing Pluto of his wife. But for this temerity he dearly paid; for, sitting on a stone to rest, he was fixed to it by bonds he could not break; nor did he get free, until Hercules tore him from the seat. On emerging from the shades he found a usurper on his throne; and not long afterwards he met his death, being flung by a false friend from the top of a high rock.

Theseus, whom the Athenians loved to regard as an historical character, is said to have consolidated the twelve petty states of Attica into a single strong commonwealth.

III. *The Argonautic Expedition.*—Phrixus and Helle, a prince and princess of Thebes, being in danger of perishing by the wicked stratagems of their stepmother, Ino, were presented by Mercury with a winged ram, whose fleece was of gold. On the back of this radiant creature they flew through the air over land and sea. The girl, having become giddy, fell into the waters of the strait afterwards called by her name. Phrixus arrived safe in Colchis at the eastern end of the Euxine, where he sacrificed the ram and hung the golden fleece in the temple of Mars. He married the daughter of the Colchian King, but was killed by that monarch in order to obtain the fleece. A young Thessalian prince of great bravery, Jason by name, then collected a warlike band in the ship *Argo*, and sailed away to recover the prize and revenge his kinsman's death. After many perils and much delay the adventurers reached Colchis. The guilty King, in the hope of causing the destruction of Jason, promised to restore the fleece, if the Grecian prince would perform certain difficult and dangerous tasks. He was to tame two fire-breathing bulls with brazen feet and horns; and, yoking them to a plough of adamant, to turn up some land never tilled before. This done, he was to sow the teeth of a dragon in the earth; and, when the strange seed had sprouted into a crop of armed warriors, he was to slay these with his single hand. And, to crown all, he was then to kill a sleepless dragon, that sat by the tree on which the fleece hung glittering. It happened that Medea, daughter of the King, fell in love with the handsome young sailor; and, being possessed of a great knowledge of poisons and magical drugs—a knowledge in which her aunt Circe was particularly skilled—she enabled her lover to accomplish the appointed tasks. When the armed men sprang up, Jason threw a stone among them, upon which they turned blade and point on one another, till the land groaned with the slain. A powerful sleeping-draught stretched the dragon in safe stupidity, and Jason carried off the fleece. The sails of the *Argo* were shaken out at once; and, when Medea's brother rashly pursued the pair, his mangled limbs were strewn along a shore, by which the father was to follow. In accordance with a kind of geography which exists in poetry alone, the *Argo* then got out of the Palus Mæotis (Sea of Azov) into certain seas, from which the voyagers could reach Thessaly only by sailing into the Mediterranean through the strait, afterwards called Gibraltar. Jason was killed by a beam, which fell from the side of the stranded *Argo*, as he lay sleeping near it; and the career of his divorced wife, Medea, full of magic, storm, blood, and terror, afforded rich material to the tragedians and poets of later ages.

IV. *The Trojan War.*—The story of the Trojan War can scarcely be regarded as a legend; but it was undoubtedly dressed with many poetical adornments.

Priam, King of Ilion, commonly called Troy, a city in the north-western part of Asia Minor, had a son called Paris, who was brought up among the shepherds of Mount Ida, and was distinguished for beauty. It happened that the three chief goddesses, Juno, Venus, and Minerva, were engaged in a contest for the golden apple, rolled by Discord among the celestial revellers, and inscribed with such words as, "Let it be given to the fairest." And to Paris the dispute was referred. He decided in favour of Venus, who promised to give him as a wife Helen of Sparta, the most beautiful woman of the age. It mattered little that she was already married to Menelaus. Paris went to Sparta, and, with or without her own consent, carried her off to Troy.

There was then a muster of the leading Grecian chiefs; for two years the land resounded with preparations; and all being complete, the allied forces assembled with their ships at Aulis in Bœotia. The oracle, being duly consulted, made response that Troy should fall, when the Grecian leaders quarrelled. A good omen also appeared, when a dragon, gliding from beneath the roots of a tree, devoured a nest with eight young birds and their mother. But unhappily Agamemnon, King of Mycenæ, and chosen chief of the armament, had killed a stag sacred to Artemis or Diana, and the wrath of the goddess was kindled. Pestilence fell on the soldiers; and calm fell on the sea. Nor did it seem that the expedition could depart, until Iphigenia, the tender daughter of Agamemnon, should be offered up to appease the enraged deity. Tempted by the pretence that she was about to be married to Achilles, the handsomest and bravest of the Grecian heroes, the girl came to Aulis; and the fatal knife was just flashing to descend with death upon its point, when the goddess carried her off in a cloud, and another victim bled in her room. Then disease abated; and a fair wind filled the sails.

For nine years the siege went on with varying fortune, Paris always refusing to restore the wife of Menelaus. In the tenth year occurred the famous quarrel, celebrated in the great epic poem called the *Iliad*.

Achilles, the Grecian hero of the war, was the son of Peleus, King of the Thessalian Myrmidons, by the Nereid Thetis. Desirous to make the boy invulnerable, his mother took him by the foot and dipped him in the River Styx. His education was intrusted to the Centaur Chiron. It happened that a beautiful girl, named Briseis, fell to his lot as part of the booty of a plundered town, when the Trojan War was well advanced; but he was obliged to give her up to Agamemnon. This so vexed him that he withdrew from the war, which then began to go against the Greeks. He remained steadfast in his resolve, until his dear friend Patroclus, who had borrowed his armour, was slain by Hector, the great Trojan prince, to whose prowess the safety of Troy was largely due. Kindled into rage, he then went forth to the war, chased Hector three times round the walls of Troy, slew him, and dragged the body at his chariot-wheels away to the Grecian ships. Achilles himself is said to have been killed before the fall of Troy by Paris, who aimed a treacherous arrow at the foot which Thetis had held, and which was the only vulnerable part of the hero.

Troy fell at last by a stratagem. Retiring to a neighbouring island, the Greeks awaited the result of the following plan. They had built a gigantic horse of wood, whose hollow interior was filled with armed men. When this was left upon the shore, a woe-begone wretch, with his hands tied behind his back, came begging admission to the city, all ringing with joy at the departure of the besiegers. His name was Sinon, and he told a piteous tale, relating how he had been doomed to death, and how he had escaped.
1184 By the advice of this deceiver the Trojans admitted
B.C. the horse within the walls, for the purpose of consecrating it to Minerva. That night Sinon undid the bolts; the freed soldiery opened the gates to their companions; rout fell upon the Trojans, and ruin upon Troy.

The wanderings and adventures of the heroes, whether victorious Greeks returning to their long-deserted homes, or defeated Trojans abandoning the ashes of their city to seek new settlements, were celebrated at great length by ancient poets, both Greek and Roman.

Agamemnon returned to Argos to find a usurper in possession of his throne and his wife. Received with apparent cordiality, he was invited to a feast, but was murdered by the guilty pair.

Ulysses after many wanderings, which are described in Homer's *Odyssey*, reached Ithaca. Assuming the disguise of a beggar, he went to his palace, and found his wife Penelope faithful amid a crowd of suitors, whom she had contrived to baffle and put off by various stratagems. Of these the most celebrated was her promise to make a choice, when a certain piece of tapestry, at which she was working, was finished: by undoing every night the portion completed on the previous day, she managed to avoid the fulfilment of her engagement.

Æneas, who carried his old father Anchises safe out of flaming Troy, supplied the poet Virgil with a theme for the great Latin epic, which narrates the stay of the wanderers with Dido of Carthage, and their fortunes in the infant settlements of Latium.

I have devoted the opening chapter of this work to the Legends of the Heroic Age, because all literature is studded with allusions to these heroes and their deeds. I have not attempted, because it falls outside the plan of these sketches, to discuss the historical probability or meaning of any of these stories; but none can help believing that there is a considerable admixture of history with their wild and beautiful poetic fancies.

The fall of Troy is commonly assigned to the year 1184 B.C.; but the chronology of this early age is not to be depended on.

CHAPTER II.

THE RETURN OF THE HERACLEIDS.

Northern Invasions.
Æolian Migration.
Dorian Migration.
The Third Harvest.
Conquest of Peloponnesus.
Fall of Argos.
The Devotion of Codrus.

IN the history of many nations we find the record of an invasion, by which hardy northern races, pouring from mountainous regions, have overswept the fertile plains and valleys of less elevated tracts, bringing new customs and new blood into the conquered lands; and, by union with the natives they have subdued, forming that mixed kind of race, by which the great work of progress has always been achieved.

It may suffice to name as examples of this in later history the barbaric inroads upon the Roman Empire—the Danish piracies, extending even to Sicily—and the Mongolian descents upon Hindostan.

Such an invasion, known as the return of the Heracleids, laid the foundation of Grecian greatness. Wave after wave the invaders came and spread, until they had occupied nearly every corner of the Peloponnesus, from which the ousted races transferred their settlements to various lands beyond the sea.

Probably sixty years after the fall of Troy the first movement in this great stirring of the races began in Epirus, where the descendants of Thessalus, a reputed son of Hercules, began to cross the chain of Pindus, and spread over the basin of the river Peneus. They rode fine horses, and easily overcame the less warlike tribes inhabiting the valleys. Some of the conquered remained in serfdom; other more adventurous spirits, and chief among them a tribe called Bœotians, pushed southward to a district, where they lingered and to which they gave their name.

Occupying a central position, they attacked, and by a hard struggle took Orchomenus and Thebes, after which the region lay at their feet. 1124 B.C. probably.

These two movements—the descent into Thessaly and the conquest of Bœotia—taken together form what is called the *Æolian Migration.*

About twenty years later the *Dorian Migration* began. From a small tract called Doris, north of Mount Parnassus, and immediately at its base, came forth a race of conquerors, who according to the popular legend were allied with the descendants of Hercules, burning through many generations to avenge the wrongs their mighty ancestor had suffered at the hands of his oppressor Eurystheus.

Here again we meet a legend, with however evidently more historic groundwork than those related in the last chapter.

It seems that the children of Hercules maintained a war in Attica with this chieftain, whom they defeated and slew. They then re-occupied the Peloponnesus. But a fierce plague drove them again to Attica ; and upon consulting the oracle they received for answer the ambiguous sentence, that after they had reaped the *third harvest* they should be re-admitted, by way of the Isthmus, into the land they had left. A son of Hercules led them to the enterprise at what seemed the fitting time ; but a hostile army blocked up the narrow way. Instead of a battle ensuing it was resolved to let a duel decide the right of entrance, on condition that, if the Heracleidan champion fell, a hundred years were to elapse before the attempt to pass should be renewed. When their champion fell, the Heracleids accordingly withdrew. But they did not keep their promise regarding the century. Twice they attempted an invasion, and twice they failed. Nor was it until the *third generation* had come, which seems to have been the true reading of the oracular response, that the invasion succeeded.

Two descendants of Hercules, Temenus and Cresphontes, assisted by Dorians, Locrians, and Ætolians, met at Naupactus, where the shores of the gulf bend towards each other and form a narrow strait. Guided by an Ætolian, named Oxylus, they crossed the water, defeated Tisamenus, the son of Orestes, and began to parcel out the Peloponnesus amongst themselves. Their guide received Elis as his pay for leading them to victory.

A brother of the Heracleidan invaders, Aristodemus by name, having been killed at Delphi by a thunderbolt before the success of the invasion, his sons claimed a share equal to what each of their uncles had got. It was agreed to decide the matter by lot. Three altars were built; and into an urn, full of water, were thrown what seemed to be three stones. Two were really stones; the third was a piece of clay which dissolved in the water. By this artifice Cresphontes managed that his lot should be last, for the stones were picked out first, and the share assigned to the last lot was Messenia, which he coveted. When the lots were drawn, on each altar was seen sitting a creature, portending the national character of the race about to spring from its representative—a toad for Argos—a writhing snake for Sparta—a cunning fox for Messenia.

1104 B.C. probably.

Gradually and not without difficulty the Dorians dispossessed the Achæans from the peninsula. The former were fewer in number, but they seem to have been hardier, better trained to war, and to have possessed in their long spears and shields that covered the whole body a decided advantage over their opponents. By establishing themselves in certain centres of ravage, much as the Danes did in the days of English Alfred, they wasted the strength of the Achæans by ceaseless harassing, until some submitted and others emigrated.

Argos, the object of the first attack, fell before the prowess of Temenus, or more probably of his successors. Cresphontes quickly overran Messenia, the prize awarded to his cunning fraud. It is likely that the conquest of Sparta cost the Dorians considerable time and trouble. Fixing their capital at Sparta on the Eurotas, they waged a war against the Achæans, whose great stronghold was the gallantly-defended and long-resisting Amyclæ, only a few miles lower down. There are reasons for supposing that it took nearly three hundred years to subdue this stubborn capital. The people of a certain town Helos on the coast made an attempt to shake off the Dorian yoke, but received a stern lesson in being deprived of all liberties political and personal, and reduced to serfdom. Hence came the despised Helots.

Several towns—Epidaurus, Troezen, Sicyon, Phlius—then fell into the hands of the Dorians; before, fixing their camp upon a hill, some eight miles off, they achieved the greater conquest of Corinth.

Aletes, the Dorian conqueror of Corinth, afterwards led an expedition against Athens, under the pressure either of ambition or famine. And thus he gave the Athenian King an opportunity of enrolling on the pages of history a name memorable among the names of patriots and martyrs. As was usual in those days, the oracle was consulted before the expedition set out; and it made answer that success should crown the Dorian arms, if the King of Athens were not killed. A Delphian, who had heard this response, made it known to Codrus, the Athenian monarch, who at once resolved to die for his country. Dressing himself like a hewer of wood, the old man went out, axe in hand, through the city gates; and wandered on, until he met two Dorian soldiers. With these he picked a quarrel, which ended in a fight. One of them sank under a stroke of his axe, but the other struck a blow fatal to Codrus but yet more fatal to the success of the Dorian expedition. When the Athenian heralds came to demand the body of their King, the outwitted invaders were struck with despair, and retreated; for, had not the oracle spoken, and who were they to strive against the gods?

It is unnecessary to recount in detail how the Dorians took Megara, which guarded the Isthmus at one end as Corinth guarded it at the other—how they occupied Ægina, and carried their conquering arms to Crete and other lands. It must suffice to say that by their migrations and conquests they altered completely the politics of the Peloponnesus, and laid the foundation of states destined to play a very prominent part in the history of Greece.

CHAPTER III.

LYCURGUS.

AMONG the Dorian states of the Peloponnesus Sparta soon rose to a prominent position; and, when the time was ripe, a man appeared, who moulded her institutions into solid form, strong and splendid. The royal family of Sparta having split into two branches, the representatives of which occupied a double throne, the younger branch produced the great lawgiver Lycurgus during the ninth century before the birth of Christ.

A story is told, which indicates the true greatness of this man. When his elder brother King Polydectes died childless, the throne fell to Lycurgus; but soon afterwards the widowed Queen bore a son. Expecting that Lycurgus would gladly seize the chance of making away with this feeble rival, she sent the baby to him, according to his own directions, given when she had made the wicked offer of conniving at the death of her own infant. Being at dinner with the leading statesmen of Sparta when the servants came in with the little child, he immediately rose from his royal seat, placed the unconscious infant there, proclaimed it King of Sparta, and named it Charilaus amid the joyous applause of all present.

The anger of the Queen and the groundless accusations of her friends compelled him to leave Sparta; and he travelled into many lands, employing himself in a close examination of the laws and customs of every place he visited. He lingered long in Crete, where the laws of Minos had sway;

and according to some accounts extended his researches to Egypt, and even to India. When he returned home, the first step he took was to consult the oracle, and, receiving a favourable answer, he began his great work of reform in the face of risks, which sometimes involved his very life.

It is a great mistake to suppose that he invented, in all the details of its wisdom, that noble system of legislation established in Sparta under his name and mainly by his agency. The germs of the constitution already existed among the Dorians, and through many years of change had been ripening slowly but surely. Taking the materials thus supplied, he reduced them into shape, and placed them upon a firm foundation.

I now proceed to give a very brief account of the Spartan constitution and system of education, as developed by Lycurgus.

One of his earliest measures was to parcel out the land upon a plan, which tended to equalize its distribution. There were two races to be cared for in this partition—the Dorians of Sparta, and the provincials, consisting partly of conquered Achæans and partly of strange settlers. The latter section of the people were the traders and manufacturers of the land. As to the Helots, the origin of whose bondage has been already adverted to, they did all kinds of drudgery, 884
public and domestic, wore a mean dress, dared not B.C.
sing a Spartan song, were often made drunk for the amusement or warning of their masters' children, and were exposed to the horrors of the *cryptia*, which sent bloodthirsty young lords roving through the land in search of the cleverest and handsomest of these slaves, whom they slew with daggers. An idea of the policy pursued towards the Helots may be gathered from a story narrated by Thucydides. When the enfeebled government of Sparta perceived certain signs, foreshadowing a rumoured insurrection of the Helots, they issued an edict that the bravest of the bondsmen should come forward and receive freedom as the due reward of their prowess in war. Two thousand were chosen for this great act of national gratitude. With garlands on their heads and joy shining in their eyes, they went from temple to temple, offering thanks to the gods: and then—how no one

but a secret few could tell—they vanished and were seen no more. Never was wholesale murder more quietly accomplished.

Before the time of Lycurgus the people had been accustomed to meet in national assembly on a certain field, and there had also existed a Senate or Council of old men, called the *Gerusia.*

The Senators numbered thirty. They were men, aged at least sixty. Amongst them sat the two Kings; and the man who, in the opinion of judges shut in a neighbouring room, received the loudest shouts on entering the place of assembly, was next in rank. The principal duty of the Senate was to prepare measures to be laid before the assembly; and they also pronounced sentence of death or degradation.

The two Kings, who neither wore finer dress nor enjoyed richer fare than the rest of the nation, acted as high priests in addition to their royal functions. To them was intrusted the consultation of the Delphic oracle and the care of the roads; but their chief prerogative in a nation of fighting men was the command of the armies. They took the principal place at all public assemblies, and were guarded by a band of one hundred men.

It is uncertain whether the *Ephors* existed before the time of Lycurgus, or were created by him or by a later statesman. They were five in number, and were elected annually. In the time of Lycurgus they were certainly not prominent in the state, affording no indication that in future times they would become supreme.

The prohibition of money, except in the form of little valueless iron bars or pieces of leather, has been ascribed to the legislation of Lycurgus; but it probably belonged to a later time.

The chief efforts of this great lawgiver were directed to the training of the young, with a view to make them vigorous and hardy. So important was this matter regarded in old Sparta, that it was the custom to lay sickly infants out in a neighbouring glen to perish by exposure. From seven to twenty years of age the boys lived under a system of public discipline. Subdivided into classes and led in both work and play by a youth, who had just emerged from this period of life, they ran, they leaped, they wrestled, they hurled the quoit, and flung the spear; they read and wrote very little, if any at all.

A thin dress in winter—a bed of rushes, pulled by themselves from the sedgy Eurotas—black broth at a public dinner-table, and but a limited supply of that—fighting with their comrades, and flogging at the altar of Artemis, till the bruised and bleeding frame would sometimes sink lifeless to the ground—prepared the Spartan boys for a life of endurance and self-denial. Their cunning was cultivated by a recognized system of stealing food from the fields and houses; praise being awarded to the successful purloiner, while blows were reserved for the bungler.

They learned to sing songs of religion and war to the music of the flute and the lyre; and in speaking, which they were trained to do only when addressed by their elders, it was expected that they would reply in a modest respectful tone and in short pithy sentences. To such a mode of speech the name *Laconic* has been therefore given ever since.

The period between twenty and thirty years of age was regarded as a time of transition from youth to manhood. Fighting on the frontier formed the chief occupation of such young freemen, who were not yet allowed to sit as members of the Assembly. When they had attained the age of thirty, the Spartans devoted themselves to the affairs of state, varying their public toils with gymnastics, hunting, and the pleasures of the common table. This kind of life lasted until the age of sixty, after which they were free from military service, and were wont to spend much of their time in the public talking-place.

The Spartan warrior, who was trained to court death rather than endure defeat, went to battle with his hair scented and garlanded, as if for a festive meeting. The strength of the Spartan armies lay in heavy-armed infantry; they were not fond of ships or of the sea, for they regarded the naval service as inferior, and left it to the Helots. The Pyrrhic dance constituted an important part of their drill; and their armies were trained to move with the perfection of a vast machine. The sternness of their discipline, and the way in which the natural feelings were repressed in the time of war, may be judged from the parting words of a Spartan mother, as she pointed to her son's shield: "Either that or on that." The coward, who flung away his shield in flight, or lost it, and lived to come home, was treated in the most contemptuous manner. A half-shaven head and a dress of ragged motley marked him out in public as one to be hustled with many jibing words, and even with kicks and blows, into the obscurest and meanest corner. No woman would marry him, if he happened to be a bachelor; and no man would marry his daughter if he had one. Shunned and degraded, he lingered out a spirit-broken existence, longing for the death he ought, according to the national opinion, to have courted on the battle-field, until perhaps the weight of his misery turned the coward into a suicide.

Thus was Sparta formed into a huge camp, full of Dorians, trained to the best methods of military service, and burning with a valour which made light of death.

When Lycurgus saw these institutions firmly rooted on Spartan soil, he adopted a stratagem to secure their continuance, which seems quite in harmony with his self-devoting patriotism. Gathering his fellow-Spartans in a public place, he made them swear a solemn oath that they would preserve his laws unchanged, until he returned from a journey upon which he was about to enter. He then set out for Delphi; sent home a response of the oracle, announcing that Sparta would certainly flourish so long as she cherished his laws; and never afterwards returned to his native land. It is uncertain when or how he died; but his name is written in letters of light upon the page of Grecian history.

When Sparta had grown strong under such fostering care, she began to cast covetous eyes on Messenia, a fair pastoral land, lying to the west, and occupied by another section of the Dorians.

A quarrel at a frontier temple by certain lakes, at which, by the Spartan account, some of their maidens were ill-treated, and, by the Messenian story, an attempt was made by beardless youths in female dress to murder some of *their* foremost citizens—and another quarrel about some kine, committed to a Spartan and by him fraudulently made away with—formed the prelude and the occasion of the First Messenian War.*

It began by the sudden seizure of Amphea, a Messenian town, whose inhabitants the Spartan invaders put to the sword. This rock-fortress, whose fine springs added much to its value, being made a centre of operations by the Spartans, some battles followed in succeeding years. But the central event of this first war was the fortification of Mount Ithomé by the Messenians. Rising high above all the surrounding eminences, and presenting a steep face on three sides, it seemed naturally marked out for a national stronghold; and round it the war began to centre and to surge.

With the story of the two Messenian wars there is a considerable admixture of legend. It is related that the Messenians sought advice from the oracle upon the fortification of Ithomé, and were told to offer in sacrifice one of their noblest girls. The father of the selected maiden carried her off; upon which Aristodemus freely offered his own child as a victim. The lover of the girl declared her unfit for the sacrifice, and Aristodemus slew her with his own hand. Being made King some time afterwards, in spite of the blood upon his hands, this warrior continued to defend his native country against its assailants. He was told to beware of Spartan cunning; and well he might dread its clever deceits. The oracle having announced that the soil of Messenia should belong to that nation which should first surround the altar of Jupiter with a hundred tripods, he set a number of workmen to make wooden ones, for they had no brass at Ithomé. However, before this could be done, a Spartan slipped into the citadel disguised as a peasant, and stealthily under cover of the darkness placed a hundred earthen tripods round the altar. This was one omen of Messenian defeat: others followed.

The suicide of Aristodemus deepened the gloom. A dream displayed to him the image of his daughter, who drew aside the folds of a black robe to show him the mortal gashes his

* This is a fitting place to mention the establishment of the Greek chronology by Olympiads. It began in 776 B.C., when an Elean named Corœbus was victorious in the games held at intervals of four years on the plain of Olympia in Elis. From this date the Greeks named each year by its place in a certain Olympiad.

own knife had inflicted; after which the spectre seemed to remove his arms, crown him with a golden circlet, and attire him in a funeral dress of white. Believing this to be a call from the grave, he went to her tomb, and died by his own hand.

The fall of Ithomé then speedily followed. The war had lasted nearly twenty years (743 B.C.—723 B.C.)

After an interval of thirty-nine years a Second War began. Of this the noble Aristomenes, born at Andania, was the hero. One of his earliest exploits was the hanging on the Brazen House at Sparta of a shield bearing an inscription, which told the wondering readers that an enemy had been among them unknown.

In their difficulty the Spartans asked advice of the oracle, and were told to seek aid from the Athenians. Already there was jealousy arising between these great rivals; and the Athenians sent the poet Tyrtæus, whom a contemptuous tradition describes as a lame school-master. Whatever he may have been, the songs of this minstrel seem to have animated the Spartans, and helped them on to victory.

The great battle of the Boar's Pillar ensued. Aristomenes in a sweeping charge drove the Spartans before him; but he rashly passed a pear-tree, on which sat unseen, according to the legend, the twins Castor and Pollux. These friends of Sparta filched his shield, which in his hurry he had dropped; and, while he was looking for it, the fugitives escaped.

The Messenians then fortified Eira, a frontier mountain in the north, as they had previously fortified Ithomé. But the fortune of war turned against them. Aristomenes, being knocked down with a stone in a skirmish, was flung with many others into a rocky ravine, from which there seemed to be no escape. All the rest were killed; Aristomenes, borne on the wings of an opportune eagle, alighted safe below. There for three days he lay waiting to die, with his face folded in his mantle. Then a sound of snuffling and pattering aroused him from a trance of patience. It was a fox that had scented the dead. Catching the beast by the tail, he followed it to a chink, through which it had crept into the pit, and soon to his joy saw a gleam of outer light. Pulling the pieces of rock out, he managed to creep through the enlarged hole, and was welcomed at Eira as one risen from the dead.

But his presence did not save his country. As before omens were sought for; and the oracle declared that, when *tragos* drank of the river, Eira should fall. Now this word had two meanings in Messenian Greek—either a he-goat or a wild fig-tree. All were trying to prevent a goat from drinking, until one day a seer observed the boughs of a fig-tree dipping into the stream. And then he knew that the omen was fulfilled, and that the destruction of Messenia was at hand.

It came in this wise. One stormy night, when frequent lightning-flashes were illuminating the ramparts of Eira, beaten with wind and rain, a Messenian soldier came home to tell his wife how the storm had driven all the sentinels under shelter, and the walls were left unguarded, under the conviction that no enemy would assault the place on such a night. The woman's lover, a Spartan herdsman, hidden in the next room, heard the words, and hurried off to apprize the Spartan leader. The assault was made amid all the tumult of thunder, wind, and lashing rain; and after a fierce resistance the Messenians were expelled from their stronghold.

Thus in 668 B.C. ended the Second Messenian War. The outcasts spread and colonized in various directions, the descendants of one band planting the name of the mother-state in Sicily, where conquered Zancle became Messene, and is still Messina.

Aristomenes died in peace at Rhodes: a legend declares that a *post mortem* examination discovered his heart to be covered with hair. The capture of Eira and conquest of Messenia certainly made Sparta the foremost state of the Peloponnesus, and prepared the way for her aspiration to supremacy over all Greece.

CHAPTER IV.

SOLON.

Attica.
Changes in the Archonate.
Draco.
The Plot of Cylon.
Solon's Stratagem.
Crissean War.
Epimenides.
Solon made Archon.
Relief of Debtors.
Four Classes.
The Four Hundred.
The Ecclesia.
The Heliæa.
Areopagus.
Death of Solon.

AFTER the patriotic death of Codrus, the nobles resolved that Athens should be governed not by Kings, but by Archons. This change however was rather, it would seem, the result of a growing tendency than a means of doing honour to the royal martyr, by putting it beyond the reach of any one to adopt the title his virtues had adorned.

Attica, destined to play so great a part in Grecian history, was a small triangular peninsula forming the south-eastern extremity of that portion of Greece north of Peloponnesus. Its soil was thin and not particularly fruitful; its silver mines and marble quarries were famous; its climate was glorious; and the watchmen on its soaring rocks looked abroad upon a sea set with islands as with jewels. It was peopled by an Ionic race, the adventures of whose hero Theseus have been already described.

Various changes took place in the Archonate, as time went on. The period of the office was limited to ten years; and at last to one. And, while the time shrank, the number of Archons increased, nine being at last annually elected from the Eupatrids or nobles. Of the nine the first was Namer of the year; the second King or Sacrificer; the third Commander of the Forces; while the others acted as Judges in the Courts of Law.

There grew up in Athens a state of social affairs, to which we shall find a striking parallel in Roman history. The middle class, consisting chiefly of merchants and farmers, got deeply in debt to the nobles, who put in force against them the law, empowering a creditor to sell as slaves a debtor and his family.

The first who attempted to remedy this evil state of things, was the Archon Draco. Publishing a system of laws, which himself described as being written in letters of blood, he endeavoured by severity to check crime. It is a popular mistake that by Draco's code every crime was punished by death, since there were lighter penalties, such as the loss of franchise and the fine of so many oxen; but petty larceny was put on a level with murder in being made a capital crime: and the tone of the whole code was unduly severe.

Between the legislation of Draco and that of Solon a great danger threatened Athens. One of the nobles named Cylon, elated by his marriage with the daughter of the *tyrant* of Megara, seized the Acropolis or citadel of Athens, and held out there for a considerable time. But food at last failed, upon which Cylon escaped. A miserable fate then befel his starving adherents, who fled for sanctuary to the temple of Athene. The Archons, afraid that the men would die of hunger in the holy place, promised them their lives if they would come out. In dependence upon this assurance they crawled feebly out, holding by a long cord, which they had tied to the statue of the goddess. So long as this bond united them to the shrine, they were safe; but unhappily the string broke, and with a shout of triumph at what seemed the withdrawal of Athene's protection, the Alcmæonids fell upon the wretches and slew them nearly all. For this crime many of the murderers were afterwards banished.

The neighbouring state of Megara about this time took the island of Salamis from the Athenians, who became so wearied out and disheartened by the failure of many attempts to recover the place, that they made a decree, condemning to death any person who should propose to make another effort of the kind.

But one day there rushed into the public place a man with disordered dress and wild eyes, wearing the aspect of a lunatic. Running to the stone, on which the heralds were accustomed to stand while making proclamation, he climbed upon it, and with impassioned gesture and fiery utterance began to chant a poem, rebuking the Athenians for their tame submission, and urging them to make another effort to regain Salamis. The crowd soon kindled into enthusiastic applause: the craven law was repealed; and preparations were made to do the bidding of the daring patriot who sang. It was Solon, the son of Execestides, a native of Salamis, whom family losses had compelled to forget the nobility of his birth, and wander as a merchant in foreign lands, seeking wealth and knowledge. Travel thus prepared him, as it had prepared Lycurgus, for the great work of legislation. Beside Solon, as he chanted his patriotic poem on that eventful day, stood a young man named Pisistratus, of whom we shall hear again. Nor was Solon content only to sing; he led his countrymen against the Megarians, and was successful in retaking the famous island of Salamis.

The Crissean War, during which Solon began to legislate for Athens, lasted ten years. The Phocian plain between Delphi and the sea was held by the Crisseans, who levied taxes not only on the merchants who came to Delphi to sell their wares, but also on the pilgrims who came to inquire of the oracle. This thinned the number of pilgrims; the Delphians complained; the Crisseans retorted with fire and sword; nor was it until a war, begun tardily by the Amphictyonic Council,* had lingered for ten years, that the covetous and sacrilegious invaders were deprived of their territory and reduced to slavery.

As a preparation for the legislation of Solon, an eminent priest and philosopher of Crete, Epimenides by name, was invited to Athens for the purpose of allaying public fears and reconciling public feuds by religious ceremonies and institutions. It is amusing to find in this ancient seer the original of Washington Irving's pleasant tale of "Rip Van Winkle;" for we are told that Epimenides one hot day, being sent by his father for a sheep, went to sleep in a cavern and did not awake for fifty years. It is gravely

* This was an assembly composed of deputies from the chief Grecian states, which met twice a year, in autumn at Pylæ and in spring at Delphi. It took especial charge of Apollo's temple at Delphi; but also gave decisions on disputed points of common politics.

stated that no one ever saw him eat; and his long mane of hair added to the awfulness of his aspect. The principal steps he took to calm the popular agitations at Athens were the appointment of a human sacrifice—the foundation of a temple to the Furies—the enactment of a check upon extravagant expenditure in religious services—and the prohibition of the strange and violent exhibitions of female grief, common at funerals. When Epimenides had done these things, the grateful Athenians desired to reward him with gold and honour; but he would receive nothing except a bough of the wild olive-tree which grew on the Acropolis, reminding the citizens of Athene to whose kindly hand tradition ascribed its presence there.

Solon, being chosen Archon, then proceeded in spite of the temptations of certain friends, who urged him to make himself tyrant of Athens, to reduce the chaos of the state into harmonious order. (1.) He relieved those hopelessly laden with debt, by reducing the rate of interest and lowering the standard of the silver coinage; he restored pledged lands to their original owners; he abolished the law of slavery for debt, and made those cruel creditors, who had sold their debtors into foreign bondage, redeem them at their own expense. (2.) He restored many to the rights of citizenship, and recalled others from exile, abolishing at the same time the blood-stained laws of Draco, except such as related to murder. (3.) Assuming wealth, not birth, as the principle of division, he placed the Athenians in four great classes—the first, containing those whose land gave them yearly 500 measures of produce; the second, those who had 300 measures a year; the third, those who had 150; the fourth, all below the last amount. The members of the first class were eligible for election to the Archonate and the chief positions in the army; the second, who were called horsemen or knights, supplied the cavalry; the third were yeomen; and the fourth, labourers.

594 B.C.

Solon instituted, or more probably re-organized the Athenian Senate, which was fixed at four hundred members, chosen from the first three classes. No one under thirty was eligible for election; and after the expiry of his year of office a member could be called to account for his conduct. The chief business of the Senate was to prepare measures, which were to be submitted to the popular assembly. The *Ecclesia*, a popular assembly, consisted of the citizens, who met once a month to discuss the affairs of national importance, laid before them by the Senate. They had the power of accepting, rejecting, or even modifying the measures submitted to them. There was a third body, the *Heliæa*, a committee of the Ecclesia, consisting of six thousand persons over thirty, who were sworn in to act as judges in matters both of fact and law. On a hill, on the western side of the Acropolis, the venerable Court of Areopagus sat in the open air, solemnly listening to appeals divested in language and manner of any trace of passion. Those who pleaded in their presence were bound by oaths of dreadful power.

Solon lived in honour until 559 B.C., engaged in the composition of a great national poem; but, before he died, he witnessed a revolution, of which an account is given in the next chapter.

CHAPTER V.

PISISTRATUS AND HIS SONS.

Three Factions.
The Body-Guard.
Twice Expelled.
A glorious Tyranny.
The Three Sons.
Daggers in the Myrtle Bush.
Hippias Expelled.
Cleisthenes.
The Corinthian Deputy.

THE handsome, rich, and free-handed Pisistratus had long been an associate and friend of Solon. He had stood by the statesman on that memorable day, when the song of feigned madness sent a thrill of patriotism through the disheartened Athenians and roused them to recover Salamis; and he had encouraged and aided the jurist in the promulgation of the famous laws, carved upon wooden pyramids that revolved in the Acropolis. But, before Solon, displeased and distracted by the many-headed factions that would not be repressed, set out upon a foreign tour, Pisistratus was already looking with ambitious eyes towards the supreme power he afterwards attained.

The physical geography of Attica cast her factions into three distinct parties:—the rich farmers of the Lowland; the merchants of the Sea-bord; and the hardy herdsmen and miners of the Highlands. Of the last Pisistratus constituted himself head.

One day he drove his chariot into the market-place of Athens, himself and his mules bleeding with recent wounds: and, when a wondering and sympathetic crowd had gathered, he related how he had been beset by a band of murderers, from whose weapons he had with difficulty escaped alive. By this piteous tale (all a fiction, for his own hand had inflicted the stabs and gashes) he obtained a guard of fifty men, bearing clubs, who always accompanied him. Solon lifted his voice against this dangerous decree; but the people were blind, and the body-guard soon swelled into a force large enough to seize the citadel. When Solon saw this, he laid his sword and shield in the street before his door, as an emblem of his utter loss of hope in the strife for liberty. But Pisistratus was soon expelled by a coalition between the party of the Plain and the powerful family of the Alcmæonids, whose exile has been already mentioned.

559 B.C.

Five years later Megacles, the head of the Coast party, offered to reinstate Pisistratus, if he would marry his daughter; a proposal which the exile accepted. Accordingly, all opposition being paralyzed in the presence of so powerful a union, Pisistratus re-entered Athens in triumph, sitting beside a tall and handsome woman clad in armour, who personated the goddess Athene bringing back her favourite chieftain to her favourite town. There may have been many in the awe-stricken crowd who believed in the real deity of the giantess. For this service, Athene—whose name was Phya—was married to Hipparchus, son of the tyrant.*

Pisistratus treated the daughter of Megacles so coldly that another coalition drove him into a second exile at Eretria in Eubœa. There he dwelt ten years, living in hope and making influence everywhere around. Thebes, Argos, Naxos aided him freely; and about twelve years after his departure he landed on the plain of Marathon, a place as yet unknown to fame. When a little later he met the forces of his foes, he fell upon them flushed with their noonday meal, some enjoying a siesta, some a game at dice, and gained an easy and complete victory, which left Athens in his hands.

Thereafter he ruled wisely and firmly for several years, lending a grace to the name of Tyrant which it has seldom worn. 'Tis true he kept bands of hired troops and a large fleet to protect his hard-won power; but these things were the necessary appendages of the revolution. He pleased the citizens by gifts of money, and by throwing open his gardens for their use; but all the while he kept them under the eye and finger of a wide-spread and vigilant police. He adorned Athens with temples; but what more than all gilded his

* It must be remembered that the word *tyrant* in Greek history has no tinge of its unpleasant modern meaning. It means the leader of a democratic revolution, or a usurper, quite irrespective of how he used his power.

name, was his desire to raise the tone of literature and learning in Greece. For this purpose he founded a library, to which the public had easy access; and he "made a collection of the poet Homer's works, superior in extent and accuracy to all that had preceded it." Thus Pisistratus atoned for the bloodshed and confusion his schemes of ambition had entailed upon Athens; and the sun of his life went calmly down at a ripe old age. His power devolved without any opposition upon his three sons, Hippias, Hipparchus, and Thessalus. 527 B.C.

Hippias the statesman, Hipparchus the man of letters, and Thessalus the brave warrior walked in the steps of their great sire, reducing taxes, encouraging literature, and fostering the resources of the state, until death overtook the second of the three. It happened thus. There were two Athenians, intimate friends, Aristogeiton and Harmodius, with the latter of whom Hipparchus had a quarrel. Instead of wreaking his grudge upon Harmodius, the son of Pisistratus put a public slight upon his enemy's sister, by refusing, when she came in her robe of ceremony to bear one of the sacred vessels, to allow her to join the procession. The friends determined to have revenge, and fixed upon the festival of the Great Panathenæa as a fitting time, since the citizens took part in the ceremonies under arms. Each of the conspirators, whom they had involved in the meshes of the plot, had a dagger hidden in the myrtle bough he carried. While the spearmen were mustering in one of the suburbs, it was noticed that a conspirator went up to Hippias, and began to speak in a low and earnest tone. Alarmed at what seemed the disclosure of the plot, Aristogeiton and Harmodius rushed away to where Hipparchus was, and struck him dead. Harmodius was instantly slain, while Aristogeiton, being taken prisoner, was afterwards put to death with tortures. Hippias then detected the rest of the conspirators by ordering all in the procession to lay aside their arms and meet him in a certain place. Those who had daggers were punished.

The policy of Hippias then became one of suspicion; and to provide a retreat in case of the worst he married his daughter to the son of the tyrant of Lampsacus.

The powerful family of the Alcmæonids, driven into exile by his father, made a great noise in Greece at this time, and gained the favour of the Delphic oracle by using marble in building the front of Apollo's temple, which they had undertaken to construct of common stone. The gratitude of the priestess caused the oracle always to respond, when Sparta came seeking an utterance, "Let freedom be restored to Athens." The reiteration produced the desired result. The Spartans invaded Attica; but Hippias, aided by a band of Thessalian horse, repelled their attack. The Spartans returned with a greater force and a greater leader, even Cleomenes, one of their kings. The Acropolis was besieged; but Hippias had so great a supply of food that the invaders were on the point of going away, when the children of the Athenian leader became their prize. This completely changed the situation. Rather than lose his little ones, Hippias evacuated Athens, and sailed away to

510 B.C.

Sigeum in Asia. The expulsion of the Pisistratids diffused joy among the foes of that great family; and the insignificant pair, to whom the slaughter of one son of Pisistratus was due, were elevated to a ridiculous renown.

Athens was then convulsed by a party struggle between Cleisthenes, chief of the Alcmæonids, and an aristocrat named Isagoras. It is needless to enter into the vicissitudes of this contest, in which the former had ultimately the advantage. He made some changes in the Athenian constitution, and is the reputed inventor of *Ostracism.**

Startled and alarmed by the growing power of Athens, the Spartans began to think that they had been wrong in expelling Hippias, and invited him to Sparta with a view of restoring him. When he came thither, deputies from the Peloponnesian states, friendly to Sparta, assembled to hear the Spartan mind upon the subject. The invasion of Attica with an allied force was mooted, but it did not chime with the feelings of the congress. None, however, ventured to object, until the deputy from Corinth rose to tell Sparta

* A method of banishment, so called from *ostrakon*, a tile or shell (on which the name was written). If six thousand citizens voted that any one was unfit to remain in Attica, that person was ostracized for ten years.

what his city had suffered from the tyrant Periander, and how shameful he thought it would appear, were Sparta to aid in forcing upon Athens a form of government utterly unlike the form she cherished and drew strength from at home. The other deputies applauded and agreed; nor was it then possible for Sparta to proceed with the design. Disappointed, Hippias went back to Sigeum, uttering prophecies of evil omen against Corinth; and we find him for many years a resident at the court of Darius the King of Persia, a country whose name now begins to be mixed intimately with that of Greece.

CHAPTER VI.

THE PERSIAN INVASIONS.

In the year 559 B.C. Cyrus, a soldier of fortune, built up the Persian Empire on the ruins of the Median throne. The conquest of Sardis, filled with the wealth of the Lydian King Crœsus, the subjugation of the Greek colonies in Asia Minor, and the capture of Babylon extended and consolidated his dominions. During the reign of his son and successor Cambyses, a daring man, named Polycrates, ruled Samos as tyrant, and upheld his power by a strong navy, which enabled him to defy even the giant power of Persia. The chief expedition of Cambyses was directed against Egypt. But it was Darius Hystaspes, whom a revolution placed upon the throne in 521 B.C., that must be looked upon as the real founder of the Persian Empire.

He undertook the invasion of Scythia or Southern Russia, upon which occasion we see for the first time in historical prominence the great soldier Miltiades.

Miltiades the Athenian, son of Cimon, received the tyranny of the Thracian Chersonesus by the death of his brother. Accompanying Darius towards Scythia, he remained behind with the other Greeks to guard a bridge which had been made over the Danube, while the Persian monarch penetrated the territory of the barbarians. During the absence of Darius, Miltiades proposed to break down the bridge and leave the Persian army to destruction. But this proposal was overruled by Histiæus, the tyrant of

Miletus; and, the bridge being loosened only at one end, Darius got safely back. Being jealous of Histiæus, the Persian monarch invited him to Susa and kept him there, leaving the tyranny of Miletus to Aristagoras. This man, having involved himself in debt by an unsuccessful attempt on Naxos, tried to excite the Ionian Greeks to insurrection.

Carrying to Sparta a brass plate, with a map of the world engraved upon it, he pointed out the Persian Empire to one of the kings, and urged him to attempt its conquest. But the incautious statement that Susa was three months journey from the sea frightened Cleomenes.

He had better fortune at Athens, whose citizens were smarting under a demand from Artaphernes, the satrap* of Sardis, that they should give earth and water, as the customary symbols of submission to the Persian rule. In compliance with the entreaties of Aristagoras, they sent twenty ships to Miletus in company with five galleys from Eretria. Sardis was burned by the allies; but the insurrection resulted in failure, Miletus being taken in the sixth year of the revolt, 494 B.C.

These events led to the invasion of Greece by a Persian army. A preliminary attempt was made by Mardonius, the son-in-law of Darius, who took the island of Thasus, valuable for its gold mines. But a storm off Mount Athos, which dispersed his fleet, and a severe loss in Thrace, which weakened his army, compelled him to abandon the enterprise. **492 B.C.**

In the year 490 B.C. six hundred triremes, with an attendant fleet of horse transports, took on board a Persian army under the command of Datis a Mede, and Artaphernes, son of the Lydian satrap and nephew of King Darius. The fleet sailed first to Samos, and then to Naxos, which yielded to the terror of its approach. When it neared the sacred isle of Delos, a panic arose among the quiet people there. But the Persians spared the place, and offered incense upon the altar. Sweeping on, the triremes next approached the Eubœan shore, where the town of Carystus rashly withstood their sum- **490 B.C.**

* The Persian governor of a province.

mons. It fell; and Eretria also, after a vain resistance, opened its gates to a destroying force.

The old traitor Hippias, who was on board a Persian ship, then pointed out the plain of Marathon as the fittest place for landing. It was the flattish basin of a small mountain torrent, rising with gentle slopes from a swampy sea-margin to a contracted glen, and measuring about five miles by two.

The Athenians, valorously resolving to give battle to the invading host encamped upon this plain, sent for aid to Sparta; but, when their swift courier reached the banks of the Eurotas, a certain superstition about the full moon caused the Spartans to do nothing until that time of the month had come. The only assistance received by Athens was from their faithful neighbours of Platæa, who came to their aid in number about six hundred heavy-armed men.

Among the ten generals in command of the Athenian army a prominent man was Miltiades, who had fled from the Chersonesus to Athens with four richly laden galleys, when threatened with a Persian invasion. A council of war being held to discuss the prudence of giving immediate battle to the Persians, the voice of this daring soldier was raised in favour of instant attack; but there were more timorous, or rather more cautious, men among the ten, who advised delay. The opinions being equally balanced, a casting vote in favour of Miltiades was given by the Polemarch Callimachus. It was the custom for each of the ten generals to hold supreme command in turn for a single day; and Miltiades waited until his own proper day of power came.

In order to make a front somewhat equal in length to that of the invading host, Miltiades was obliged to withdraw a great many troops from his centre and add them to the wings. The centre of the little Athenian army was therefore broken and pursued by the Persians, while the stronger wings, driving the crowds of Asiatics in rout before them, closed in upon the victorious Persians, who had pierced their centre, and put them too to flight. The Persians fled to their ships, the Greeks following in hot pursuit. Seven vessels were captured; and so keen was the struggle that a certain Greek hero laid hold of the side of a Persian ship and did not let go until an axe had lopped his wrist. The numbers, usually assigned to the contending hosts, are one hundred and twenty thousand on the Persian side against ten thousand on the side of Greece.

When the battle was over, a body of Spartans arrived; but there was nothing to do. They went, however, to survey the field of Marathon, strewn with Persian dead.

The influence of Miltiades now grew so great that he induced the Athenians to fit out seventy triremes to punish some of the islands. Leading the fleet first to Paros, to gratify, it was said, a private grudge, he there received an injury in knee or hip, which ended in gangrene and death. On his return a charge of deception was brought against him by a political foe, and a fine of fifty talents was imposed. Being unable to pay this sum, he went to prison, where he died.

Xerxes, son of Darius, became King of Persia in 485 B.C. He was a weak and voluptuous prince, upon whose fancy certain traitorous Greek exiles, aided by the false prophecies of Onomacritus, wrought so skilfully that he resolved to invade Greece. After four years of preparation all was ready. A double bridge, formed of anchored ships, spanned the Hellespont, where it is nearly a mile broad; and the lofty headland of stormy Athos was severed from the mainland by a canal.

At length the marvellous procession began to move like a riband of gold and steel and bright-dyed dresses from Sardis to Abydos. Each nation wore its own distinctive armour and weapons. The Persian bow and spear and dagger were varied by the Sacian hatchet and the Chaldean club; and amid the calico tunics of India, the striped raiment of Arabia, and the goat-skins of the mountaineers, glittered grotesquely the white and red paint, with which the Ethiopians daubed the breast and limbs left unclothed by their mantles of leopard-skin. In a chariot (when the sun did not shine too strongly) sat Xerxes in god-like state; and behind him, their lances tipped with gold and silver, marched the ten thousand Immortals, the flower of the Persian host. Thus grandly they approached the bridge.

After a review the Immortals led the way across, treading upon myrtle boughs; and for a week by night and day the stream of living creatures poured on,—horse and foot, white and black, dromedary and wild ass, baggage-truck and sumpter-mule. Xerxes then proceeded, not to *number* his army, but to *measure* it like so much corn. Causing 10,000 men to assemble, he formed a ring fence round them, and into this he packed successive bands, until he had reached an end. The number is stated at 1,700,000 foot and 80,000 horse; while his fleet consisted of 1207 vessels.

The host then marched through Thrace, drinking the rivers as it passed, according to a striking hyperbole. Varying the monotony with human sacrifices, it proceeded along the shore to Mount Athos, where the army struck inland across the peninsula of Chalcidice.

Athens and Sparta stood almost alone in this hour of extreme peril to Greece. Fear or jealousy had chilled any patriotism which Thessaly, Phocis, Thebes, and Argos might have had. But by the Eurotas and the Cephisus there were found great men equal to the occasion. Leonidas was King of Sparta in room of Cleomenes; and on the grave of dead Miltiades stood Themistocles the Keen, and Aristides the Just.

Taking advantage of the rivalry between the Athenians and the people of Ægina, Themistocles had induced his countrymen to devote the rent of the silver mines of Laurion to the equipment of a worthy fleet. The addition of a hundred ships accordingly raised the number of their navy to two hundred; and it was further decreed that twenty new triremes should be built every year. Thus it happened that Athens, without intending it, was ready for the coming galleys of Persia.

A congress of Grecian states, held at the Isthmus of Corinth, exerted itself to rouse the laggard and the timorous: with but slight success. Gelo, the powerful tyrant of Syracuse, who at any time could muster a larger force than any of the states at home, offered indeed to send a great army, on condition of being raised to the chief command; but the Spartan envoys indignantly refused to accept aid from a Sicilian Greek on such terms.

It was at first resolved to withstand the Persian host at Tempe, but the position was found untenable. While the

Grecian fleet therefore took post to the number of two hundred and seventy-one ships at Artemisium under the command of Eurybiades, a Spartan, a military force assembled at Thermopylæ.

This was a pass four or five miles long, between the rocky shoulder of Callidromus and the curving shore of the Maliac Gulf, which then ran much further inland than it runs at present. Deep mud on one side and steep rock on the other left but a narrow causeway between. The name Thermopylæ, signifying *Hot Gate*, was derived from a warm sulphur spring, that gushed from the base of the mountain.

This position was occupied by Leonidas, the Spartan King, with three hundred of his subjects, and scarcely five thousand men from other states and cities. The Greeks took the matter so coolly that it was not thought necessary to put off the Olympic games, and the nine days' Spartan festival of the Carnean Apollo.

Upon his arrival at the place Leonidas heard for the first time that there was a mountain-path, by which a force might pass over Callidromus and attack him in the rear. To guard this he posted a band of Phocians among the hills.

Many of the Greek defenders of this pass felt their hearts sink, when they saw the numberless spear-heads of the Asiatic host glittering in the plain, and would have retreated in panic but for the persuasive words of Leonidas. It never occurred to the mind of Xerxes that this small band would dare to withstand the myriads of his host; he accordingly halted until fear should melt them away. Surprised at their remaining, he then sent a horseman to see what they were doing; and this man, approaching as near as he could safely, brought back word that some of the Spartans were engaged in gymnastics, and that others were sitting by the wall combing their hair. This Xerxes was assured meant that they were preparing for battle; but he could not believe in such foolhardiness (as it seemed to him) until he had waited four days more and found the defenders of the pass still biding by the wall.

On the fifth day, seating himself on a throne, he sent some Medes and Cissians to the attack. Advancing with a narrow front owing to the confined nature of the ground, these soldiers, whose short spears could not reach the living wall of Greeks, were again and again beaten back in broken masses. Not a whit more success crowned the onset of the Immortals, before whom the Greeks would sometimes flee a few yards in order to return with irresistible force upon the straggling files. The Persian despot, when he saw these daring foreigners playing with the prowess of his chosen troops, and slaughtering them in heaps, could not help more than once starting in dismay from the throne, on which he had seated himself in the certainty of success. Next day the same things happened.

But a traitorous Greek, named Ephialtes, a native of that place, informed Xerxes of the path called Anopæa, which led across the mountains; and the Immortals under their leader Hydarnes, starting at dusk, marched all night, and, guided by Ephialtes, reached the summit of the path about dawn. Before the day broke, a sound of many feet rustling in the leaves attracted the attention of the Phocians on guard. When they saw the Persians, these Greeks, expecting an attack, moved aside from the path to a more commanding position; but the Immortals, intent on a higher enterprise than their defeat, marched steadily by and descended towards the rear of the Grecian host.

There being time for a retreat, Leonidas permitted those of his little band who wished to depart to do so. Honour compelled the Spartans to die where they stood; the seven hundred Thespians remained to share their fate; and the four hundred Thebans were detained as hostages. A striking instance of the Spartan spirit was afforded by the answers of two friends, whom Leonidas wished to bear letters for him to Sparta. They would not go; one saying that he came to carry arms, not letters, while the other said that his deeds would be a sufficient message to Sparta.

Then the struggle began. Leonidas led his men out to meet the hordes of Xerxes, who were whipped on to the contest with the scourges of their officers. Needing no such ignominious stimulant, the gallant suicides flung themselves upon the Persian spears, selling their lives as dearly as they could. The sea was thick, and the ground was heaped with the Persian dead, when the Immortals entered the southern outlet of the Pass. The Greeks then retreated with broken weapons and limbs smeared with dust and blood to a hillock behind the wall. And there to a man they died under a pitiless rain of arrows, spears, and stones. It happened that two Spartans were absent from the band with disease of the eyes, when the path across the hills was made known to the Persians. One of them was led by a slave to die at his post; the other, Aristodemus by name, went home, but was ever afterwards sneered at as a coward, and shunned like a leper.

480 B.C.

Meanwhile what of the fleet? The peaks of Sciathus, an island to the east, grew bright with beacon-fires as soon as the advanced squadron of the Persian fleet appeared. Just then a timely storm strewed the shore of Magnesia with dead and driftwood,—a disaster which checked the Persian advance for a while. A squadron of two hundred ships was sent to take the Greeks in the rear by sailing into the southern end of the Euripus, while the mass of the Persian navy anchored at Aphetæ. A diver having brought word of these things to the Greek admiral, he resolved to face the foe. The little Greek fleet was soon encompassed in what seemed a fatal embrace by a vast circle of Persian galleys; but the inner ring, turning sharp prows outward, suddenly expanded, like rays shooting from a centre, and cleft the Persian lines into shattered fragments. A second storm wrecked the squadron that was despatched to make an attack on the rear; and the Persian crescent was shattered a second time by the ardent and skilful sailors of Greece. But triumphs like these were too exhausting; and the sadly glorious news, borne by a swift galley from Thermopylæ, decided the necessity of a retreat.

From Thermopylæ Xerxes led his troops to Delphi, attracted by the wealth of the shrine. The people went to the caves of Parnassus, leaving the protection of the temple to the gods. And Greek superstition was both rejoiced and awe-stricken, when thunderbolts struck the crags, below which the Asiatics were marching, and hurled crushing masses on the crowded ranks.

Meanwhile the Peloponnesians were hard at work fortifying the Isthmus with a wall.

The Persian force then pressed on to Athens, burning Thespiæ and Platæa by the way. The oracle had given response to the inquiring Athenians that they should be saved by a *wooden wall;* and opinions were divided as to the meaning of this phrase. The young men thought it meant the fleet; the older citizens called to mind a thorny hedge round the rock of Pallas, and desired that this should be strengthened as a barricade. Certain omens, among which the chief was the disappearance of the sacred snake that ate its sweet cake in the temple every month, seemed to menace ruin. The advice of Themistocles was finally taken. Salamis, Ægina, Troezen received the families and goods of the citizens, while the bulk of the fighting-men went on board the fleet, now increased to three hundred and eighty ships.

When Xerxes came to Athens, he found a few citizens on the Cecropian Hill inside the wooden wall, in which *they* placed their trust. And for some time they resisted, rolling heavy stones from the summit, and quenching the flames, when fiery arrows, shot from the Areopagus, kindled the wood. But the Persians effected an entrance by scaling the northern rocks; and a scene of flame and slaughter followed. Hope however was rekindled among the Athenian survivors, when they saw a green shoot, which had sprung in one night to the height of a cubit from the charred trunk of the olive-tree, sacred to Pallas.

Taking counsel with the wise Mnesiphilus, Themistocles urged the assembled admirals to give battle to the Persian fleet within the narrow strait of Salamis; and, when Adeimantus the Corinthian objected with insulting words, he threatened that the Athenians would sail away and found a colony in Italy. This decided the acceptance of his plan.

The Persian fleet, coming to anchor in the bay of Phalerum, and blocking the Greek ships up apparently with the certainty of destroying them, caused the murmurs of the Peloponnesians to grow loud again. Themistocles met the murmurs by stratagem. Sending a slave skilled in the Persian tongue to Xerxes, he bade that monarch hem in the Greeks by night, since they were sure to turn their prows against one another in their rage and fear. This message, delivered from Themistocles as if from a secret friend, caused a movement of the Persians, which blocked up both ends of the narrow channel in which the Greek ships lay. The news of this movement was brought to the Greek council by Aristides, who three years earlier had been banished by *ostracism*, and who came by night from Ægina to bear the tidings to his rival Themistocles.

The Greeks were thus forced to fight in the Strait of Salamis. Xerxes, surrounded by scribes to chronicle the valour of his captains, took his seat upon a throne erected upon one of the neighbouring headlands. Themistocles encouraged the Greeks by a speech. Backing their ships until the Persians were in the narrowest portion of the strait, where their whole extended front could not come into action, the Greeks began the contest by an Athenian galley darting forward to strike a Persian ship. The example was quickly followed. So skilfully had the place and time been chosen by the wily Athenian admiral, that the advantages of the Persians were turned into positive evils. Their *number* huddled them almost helplessly in the narrow channel; their *size* caused them to catch the full force of a strong wind, which was blowing up the strait at the hour of engagement. Aristides, who looked on from the shore, rendered signal service to the cause of Greece by carrying a band of troops to the island of Psyttaleia at the southern entrance of the strait, and falling on the confused Persians crowded together there.

The defeat of Salamis sent Xerxes home. In order to secure the bridge he despatched the fleet northward without delay; and it gives us a striking idea of how quickly and how much the Persian crews had learned to fear Grecian ships, when we find them one dark night, off Cape Zoster, scattering in flight before some tall rocky islands, which they mistook for the galleys of the foe. Mardonius had offered to remain in Greece, and "complete its subjugation," if Xerxes would leave him three hundred thousand men. The Persian monarch was pleased to accept the offer; and the retreat began.

Hunger and disease ravaged the broken host, as it hurried northward. At the Strymon the breaking of the ice plunged many in a watery grave. And, when the Hellespont was reached, it was found that a storm had broken down the bridge. But the fleet had arrived; and the wearied and beaten Persians, who survived, found rest at Abydos.

Mardonius, who had accompanied Xerxes to Thessaly, spent the winter there, and then moved to Athens. On his approach the citizens carried their families over to Salamis, and left the city to its fate. When messengers from Athens sought aid at Sparta, there was considerable delay in granting it. At length five thousand men, each attended by seven helots, set out under Pausanias, upon which Mardonius retreated to Bœotia.

The Grecian army, amounting to nearly one hundred and ten thousand men, encamped at Erythræ on the roots of Mount Cithæron, but in a position badly supplied with water. Here there was a skirmish of cavalry and archers, which resulted in the repulse of the Persians, and the death of their gold-mailed captain; in grief for whom his troopers shaved their heads and their horses, filling all the land with their lamentations. After this Pausanias led his army to the banks of a stream near Platæa, and there prepared for battle—the Lacedemonians holding the right wing, the Athenians the left. And so the armies lay for some days, until one night a horseman, Alexander of Macedon, came to the Athenian pickets and told the generals that Mardonius meant to fight next day, and that the Persians had but little food. The capture of a spring, on which the Spartans depended, obliged the Grecian army to move to Platæa. The Persians followed, and commenced to rain arrows on the Spartans, who, because the sacrifices were unfavourable, sat for a long time as living targets for the Persian archers. At last prosperous signs appeared. The wicker shields of the Persians, their slight armour, and short spears could not resist the Spartan rush. Mardonius, riding on a white horse and gleaming with gold, received his death-wound, and the Persian army fled in fragments. The Asiatic camp was then stormed chiefly by the prowess of the Athenians, and rich booty rewarded the captors.

On the same day the Greeks won another victory on the promontory of Mycale, opposite the southern end of Samos.

When the Grecian fleet under Leotychides moved thither from Delos, they found a Persian army of sixty thousand arrayed on the shore, guarding the galleys, which were drawn up on the sand and surrounded with a palisade. Standing on the platform of his galley, the Grecian admiral shouted to the Ionians on shore to be true to their promise and to remember the given watchword; a *ruse* which excited in the mind of the Persian leader suspicions of the Asiatic Greeks. Landing, the Greeks advanced to the attack in two divisions, the Athenians and others proceeding by the flat shore, while the Spartans struggled more inland across ravine and ridge. Reaching the barricade first, the Athenians had pierced it, and were still contending with the Persians, routed but resolute, when the Spartans came up to decide the issue of the fight. Only a handful brought to Xerxes the news that the terrible Greeks had crossed the sea to smite his soldiers in their own position, on their own shore.

The chief remaining events of the war were a movement of the Grecian fleet to the Hellespont for the purpose of breaking the bridge, already destroyed, as they found, by storms; and the reduction of the Chersonese, which the Athenians accomplished by the successful siege of Sestos.

It now remains that I should conclude this outline by telling what became of Themistocles and Aristides, the most prominent Athenians of the time.

The former, a wily and unscrupulous politician, caused the Athenians to surround their new city with a strong wall. To this the Spartans objected, as they said, because it would afford a safe stronghold to the Persians if they came back, but in reality through fear of Athens growing too strong. Themistocles went in person to Sparta, quietly telling his colleagues in the embassy not to start until the wall had reached a certain height. And then every person in Athens, capable of handling a trowel or carrying a load, was set to work at the wall, for which even the stones of the tombs were used. Themistocles at Sparta postponed all business until the arrival of his colleagues; upon which the Spartans sent to Athens other envoys, whom Themistocles desired his countrymen to detain. When the wall had reached a useful height, the cunning Athenian made known the true state of affairs, and the outwitted southerns were compelled to put the best face they could on their discomfiture.

Themistocles also caused his countrymen to fortify the harbour of Piræus. By his indecent haste to be rich he made enemies at home; by his efforts to strengthen Athens he excited the hatred of powerful states abroad; and chiefly owing to the machinations of Sparta he was (471 B.C.) ostracised—a just retribution for having brought the same fate on Aristides. He went first to Corcyra (Corfu) and then to Epirus, where through the contrivance of his host's queen he gained the protection of Admetus, King of the Molossians, by sitting at the hearth with the royal baby in his arms. Unable to shelter him permanently, Admetus helped him to reach Pydna in Macedonia, whence he sailed to Ephesus, encountering by the way the perils of storm and capture. It is said that he travelled to the Persian court in a close litter under a lady's name. Sending a letter to Artaxerxes, he reminded the monarch that he had been instrumental in saving the Persian fleet after the battle of Salamis, and, promising that after a year of study he would announce a plan of action fraught with glory to the Persian arms, he insinuated himself into the King's favour to such an extent as to rouse the envy of the courtiers. Three cities were assigned for his support, and in one of these, Magnesia in the basin of the Mæander, he died before the publication of the promised plan.

The less brilliant though equally great Aristides signalized his later life by consolidating the Ionian confederacy, and lifting Athens to the head of that great organization. In conjunction with Cimon, the son of Miltiades, he commanded the Athenian squadron in the fleet, which remained for some time under the control of Pausanias the Spartan. But Pausanias grew arrogant and began to ape the Persian modes of life, thus indicating a leaning which ultimately involved him in a secret and traitorous correspondence with Xerxes. His severity and affectation disgusted and estranged the Ionians, who therefore invited Athens to take the lead in the confederacy. The aims of this union were "to protect the Greeks in the islands and the coasts of the Ægean from the aggressions of the Persians, and to weaken and humble the barbarians." To the calm and sagacious Aristides was confided the task of apportioning the contributions required from the several members of the confederacy; and he fulfilled the difficult duty with rare success, exciting no murmurs and incurring no suspicions. Some gave money; stronger states equipped ships; 460 talents formed the entire annual assessment; and Delos was chosen to be the treasury and place of congress.

When Sparta sank to a subordinate place, she withdrew her forces from the confederacy, and became once more the head of the Peloponnesian states—a step which placed her in distinct rivalry with Athens. The democratic tendencies of the latter were increased, when Aristides caused the *Thetes*, the fourth class of citizens, out of which the sailors of the fleet were chiefly drawn, to become eligible for the Archonship.

These works done, Aristides faded obscurely out of history and of life, leaving no riches but a spotless memory and name behind.

A few words will dismiss the traitorous Pausanias. Fallen from his high position and smarting under the disgrace of a public trial, he formed a plot to raise the helots in revolt, and with Persian aid make himself master of Sparta. His practice was to send letters to the satrap, containing a postscript that the bearer was to be put to death. One of the emissaries, suspecting mischief, opened the letter, much as Shakspere makes Hamlet do during the voyage to England, and, finding his intended doom written there, disclosed the treachery of Pausanias to the Ephors. They, concealed behind a thin boarding, heard the guilty man commit himself in conversation with his former confederate; and measures were taken to arrest him. Warned of this, he fled to the brazen temple of Athene; but they were resolved that he should not escape. The roof was taken off; the doorway blocked with stones, one of which his own mother patriotically placed in the entrance. And there he starved to death, being carried out just when the last breath was leaving his lips, lest his corpse might defile the holy place.

GREAT NAMES OF GRECIAN LITERATURE, &c.

FIRST PERIOD.

HOMER, great epic poet—an Asiatic Greek—born probably at Smyrna or Chios before 850 B.C.—said to have been a blind minstrel—works, the *Iliad* and the *Odyssey*. There has been much controversy about the authorship of these. They were probably framed from the floating lays of the Trojan war by Homer; and then, falling into scattered fragments in course of time, were collected in *writing* by Pisistratus the Athenian.

HESIOD, a poet—born at Ascra in Bœotia—lived about 735 B.C.—chief works, *Works and Days*, a collection of precepts, and *Theogony*, upon the origin of the world and the gods—spent the end of his life at Orchomenos.

ARCHILOCHUS, (probably 714-676 B.C.)—belonged to Paros—a lyric poet, and the earliest writer of iambic verses—noted for satiric power—fell in battle with the Naxians.

ALCÆUS, (flourished about 611 B.C.)—a lyric poet of Mitylene in Lesbos —famed for his warlike *Odes*—said to have invented the Alcaic metre.

SAPPHO, (flourished about 600 B.C.)—a lyric poetess of Lesbos—said to have leapt, through love of Phaon, from a rock—extant work *Ode to Aphrodite* (*Venus*).

SUSARION, native of Megara—originator of the *Attic Comedy*, which he introduced between 580-564 B.C.

ÆSOP, lived about 570 B.C.—the slave of a Samian, who gave him freedom—flung from a precipice at Delphi—author of *Fables* in prose, but not of those now bearing his name.

ANACREON, (probably 563-478 B.C.) born at Teos in Asia Minor—a celebrated lyric poet—lived chiefly at Samos and Athens—the *Odes*, ascribed to him, are said to be spurious.

THESPIS, (flourished about 535 B.C.)—native of Icarus in Attica—an actor, who so improved the old tragedy that he has been called the father of Greek Tragedy.

PYTHAGORAS, (flourished between 540 and 510 B.C.)—a native of Samos, distinguished as a philosopher—travelled in Egypt and the East—taught the transmigration of souls—skilled in arithmetic and music—settled at Crotona in Italy—either burned there in the temple by a mob, or driven into exile, upon which he starved himself to death. Pythagoras of Rhegium (480-430 B.C.), was a celebrated sculptor.

ÆSCHYLUS, born at Eleusis in Attica, 525—died at Gela in Sicily, 456 B.C.—fought at Marathon and Salamis—the earliest of the great Attic tragedians—left Athens for Syracuse, when defeated by Sophocles—seven plays extant, the *Persians, Seven against Thebes, Suppliants, Prometheus, Agamemnon, Choephori, Eumenides.*

EPICHARMUS, (about 540–450 B.C.)—born in the island of Cos—lived chiefly at Megara in Sicily, and at Syracuse—noted as a writer of *Comedy*, into which he introduced a regular plot.

PINDAR, (about 522–442 B.C.)—born at Cynoscephalæ near Thebes—noted as a great lyric poet—wrote hymns, pœans, dirges, and poems of other kinds, but the only works we have entire are his *Epinicia*, choruses to commemorate triumphs in the public games.

SECOND PERIOD.

CHAPTER I.

PERICLES.

Cimon.
Disaster at Sparta.
Sketch of Pericles.
Contest for Popularity.
Victory of Pericles.
Tanagra.
Thirty Years' Truce.
Glory of the Age.
Phidias Accused.
Last Days of Pericles.

CIMON, the son of Miltiades, of whom mention has been already made, now rose to prominence at Athens. The fine of 50 talents, which had been imposed upon his father and for which he became liable, was paid by a wealthy Athenian, who had been fascinated by his sister's beauty.

In 466 B.C. the Athenians repressed a revolt in Naxos; and in the same year Cimon won a distinguished victory over the Persian fleet and army at the mouth of the river Eurymedon in Pamphylia, where after sinking their ships by scores he followed them to their tents and took possession of their treasures. He afterwards overran the Thracian Chersonese, of which his illustrious father had once been tyrant.

Meanwhile in 464 B.C. a terrible blow fell on Sparta. The noblest of her young men were exercising in a public building, when the shocks of an earthquake were felt, and the toppling walls crushed them to death. At the same moment the summits of Taygetus were riven; enormous blocks of stone rolled thundering down; and nearly every house in Sparta either sank into the sudden chasms of the earth or was reduced to heaps of ruin. This not only prevented the Spartans from sending aid to Thasos, which was hard pressed by an Athenian force, but otherwise crippled the movements of the state. To add to their perplexities the Third Messenian War began. Ithome was fortified; and many helots and discontented free Laconians joined the revolted garrison. 464 B.C.

Pericles, the rival of Cimon and the most brilliant of Athenian statesmen, was now rising above the horizon. As the son of Xanthippus, who led the victorious Athenians at Mycale, and of Agariste, a descendant of Cleisthenes, the youth had illustrious blood in his veins. But greater than advantages of blood and birth were the intellectual gifts, which he cultivated with ceaseless industry. His chief teacher, the moulder of his philosophic opinions and the inspirer of his eloquence, was Anaxagoras; but he also studied dialectics under Zeno, and music under Damon. He was sweet-voiced and handsome, but had a head so much too long as to attract the jeers of the comic poets, among whom he was nicknamed "Onion-pate," and was bantered as being evidently the *Head* of the state. Hence his statue was always carved with a helmet to hide the defect.

Such was the man who now began to lead the democratic party in Athens in opposition to Cimon, the chief of the aristocrats. It was but a revival of the old rivalry between Themistocles and Aristides.

They adopted different plans to secure the favour of the citizens. Cimon, who was rich with the prize-money of the Persians, scattered his wealth with a lavish hand. He built the south wall of the citadel—filled the marshes between the city and her harbours with masses of masonry, on which walls were afterwards to rise—and planted groves and avenues of trees to beautify the city. All might pluck the fruit of his orchards, round which no fences ran; any member of his *deme* could dine any day at his table; and, if an old citizen passed, shivering in a thin mantle, one of his attendants pressed a warm cloak on the poor fellow, often slipping some coins at the same time quietly into the shaking hand. Pericles, who had a moderate fortune and was nobly economical, took another way to please the citizens. Regarding the public money as the property of all the people, he caused the poorer citizens to receive from the treasury an allowance, which enabled them to attend the theatre; and he also secured payment for loss of time to the jurors who attended the courts of justice. Personally he devoted all his time to work, being never seen in the street except between his home and the place of council; no party of pleasure could attract him to its festive circle; and his speeches were so carefully prepared that he never spoke an unconsidered word. Such a man, so devoted to his country's welfare, and so calm and unruffled in his demeanour, that from his placid temper insults fell like pointless darts from armour, exercised remarkable influence in the state.

In 461 B.C. the Athenians sent a force under Cimon, the friend of Sparta, to aid the Spartans in besieging Ithome. But, the siege not advancing, the Spartans began to suspect that the Athenians were wilfully slack, and sent them away. This broke the alliance between the states; and Athens made a treaty with Argos, a power hostile to Sparta.

Pericles then, with the aid of his friend Ephialtes, struck a heavy blow at aristocracy in Athens, by stripping the ancient court of Areopagus of nearly all its authority and jurisdiction. This portended the fall of Cimon, who had been previously impeached for not invading Macedonia, but had been acquitted. Now he was ostracised as an enemy of the people; and Pericles held sole sway at Athens, the opposition of Thucydides soon ceasing to affect his position.

The Athenian party at Megara admitted an Athenian garrison into that city, by which means Athens came to be embroiled in a war with Corinth, then at variance with Megara. About the same time an Athenian expedition went into Egypt to fight with the Persians: this afterwards turned out disastrously.

During the Corinthian War, beginning in 457 B.C., Ægina took part against Athens. The hero of the struggle was the soldier Myronides, who defeated the Corinthians with great loss.

Athens and Sparta now came into warlike collision. It happened on this wise. The Phocians having invaded Doris, the cradle of the Spartan race, the Spartans sent a force against them. It was successful; but there seemed difficulties in the way of returning home. As if to meditate on the matter, the Spartan leader diverged into eastern Bœotia and encamped at Tanagra on the borders of Attica. Taking this to mean war, an Athenian army advanced, and soon engaged. The desertion of some Thessalians so weakened the Athenians that they gave way. Pericles was in the battle; and Cimon would have been, had the Five Hundred permitted him to fight. But their suspicions of his friendship for Sparta were too strong. He took a noble way of rebuking their distrust, when he left his armour with his friends as a centre round which they were to fight. At the end of the day a ring of corpses and wounded men round the blood-stained arms told how well those friends had fulfilled their trust. The Athenians made up for this disaster by routing the Bœotians, three months later, among the vineyards of Œnophyta. This achievement of Myronides secured for them the chief sway in Bœotia.

The Third Messenian War ended in 455 B.C.; and the Messenian garrison of Ithome, allowed to leave Peloponnesus with their children, were placed by the Athenians at Naupactus on the northern side of the narrow entrance to the Corinthian Gulf.

The temper of the Athenians having changed, Pericles then moved that Cimon be recalled; and he was reinstated as a citizen of Athens. Having soon afterwards led an armament to Cyprus, he received a wound of which he died, 449 B.C.

The Athenian cause in Bœotia was severely shaken by the battle of Coronea, two years later. A rash general, named Tolmides, led a force to chastise the exiles who had seized certain cities there; but lost his army and his life in the attempt. The immediate consequence of this was the revolt of Eubœa, to which Pericles went with a band of men. But the news of an invasion of Attica by a Peloponnesian army brought him back in haste. He averted this danger by bribing the leader, and then went back to reduce the revolted islanders to allegiance. And then was concluded between the rival states, Athens and Sparta—scarcely yet ready to plunge into the deadly war already foreshadowed in their history—a truce for thirty years.

445 B.C.

This breathing-time permitted Pericles to devote his attention to those works of architecture, which made Athens the most beautiful city of ancient times, whose temples are still, even in their ruins, models for the public buildings of our modern centres of civilization. Aided by his friend Phidias, the great sculptor, he erected the Parthenon and the Propylæa; which with other buildings always in view filled the mind of an Athenian with the grandeur of the state as contrasted with any personal glory that might cling round individual names. Under his fostering care the Greek drama also brightened at Athens to a lustre, which has never grown dim. Nor was he engaged entirely in works of art and literary patronage. Sensible of the evils of over-population, he drained off the poorer citizens and those of more enterprising spirit to various colonies, which strengthened Athens abroad and relieved her at home.

His principal military exploit at this time was the reduction of Samos. When the people of that place refused, at the command of the Athenians, to cease from war with Miletus, Pericles by force established a democratical constitution in the island. The Samians soon revolted; and he then besieged the city. The Samian prisoners were branded on the brow with a ship, while those Athenians, who were taken, were marked with the figure of an owl. During a cruise of Pericles the Samians obtained some advantages; but on his return, by building a wall and using heavy battering engines, he reduced the city after nine months' siege. Many were the garlands showered on him by fair Athenian hands, as he descended from the platform after pronouncing the funeral oration of those countrymen who had fallen in the war.

The enemies of Pericles struck at him through those whom he loved. The sculptor Phidias, who executed the ivory statue of Athene, was accused of having appropriated some of the gold, of which its massy ornaments were made. This charge was met by proposing to take the gold off and weigh it: and so the accusation fell to the ground. The accusers then shifted their attack. Perceiving on the shield of the goddess in the sculptured battle with the Amazons a bald old man lifting a stone, whose face resembled that of Phidias, and a figure whose hand with lifted spear half concealed a striking likeness of Pericles, they loudly raised the cry of impiety; and on this charge Phidias was flung into prison, where he sank under disease. Aspasia, the mistress, and Anaxagoras, the tutor of Pericles, were also accused. The former was acquitted at the instance of Pericles, who even wept before her judges; the latter went into exile.

In the following chapter will be narrated what Pericles did during the Peloponnesian War, in the third year of which he died. It remains for me briefly to describe that event. A desolating plague deprived him of a worthless eldest son, and of nearly all his friends and counsellors; but his granite face gave no sign of woe or perplexity. At last however Paralus, his younger son and the darling of his old age, fell a victim to the sickness. Nature could bear no more. As he was laying the funeral wreath upon the cold brow, he burst into a passion of tears, and cried out bitter words of anguish that could not be concealed. The plague soon mercifully smote himself with its lingering tortures. As he lay scarcely able to speak, he showed a friend, who came to see him, a little charm hung by some woman's hand around his neck; and a feeble smile at his own weakness flitted over his wasted face. Those who sat about his dying bed were talking of his deeds in war and policy, when the still figure, supposed to be unconscious, gasped out that they were forgetting his noblest praise—"That no Athenian through his means had ever put on mourning."

429 B.C.

CHAPTER II.

THE PELOPONNESIAN WAR.

Causes of the War.	Alcibiades.	Battle of Notium.
Invasions of Attica.	Socrates.	Ægos-potami.
Platæa.	Battle of Mantinea.	Surrender of Athens.
Sphacteria.	Sicilian Expedition.	The Thirty Tyrants.
Battle of Delium.	Siege of Syracuse.	Revolution.
Peace of Nicias.	The Naval War.	Death of Alcibiades.
Cleon.	Return of Alcibiades.	Death of Socrates.

THE prelude of the Peloponnesian War was an outbreak of hostility between Corinth and her colony Corcyra. The latter had grown to be a naval power second only to Athens. A colony of Corcyra—the Illyrian town of Epidamnus (the modern Durazzo)—being refused aid from the mother-state, appealed to Corinth, and received it. Incensed at this, the Corcyreans laid siege to the town. There was then a sea-fight in the Gulf of Ambracia, which proved disastrous to the Corinthians; and on the same day Epidamnus surrendered.

Athens then made a defensive alliance with Corcyra; and in an important naval action that took place near the Thesprotian Gulf the Athenian galleys took a part.

This collision between Athens and Corinth led to the revolt of Potidæa on the Isthmus of Pallene, a colony of Corinth, but a subject-ally of Athens. The Athenians, having gained a victory at Olynthus, a few miles off, then formed the siege of Potidæa, 432 B.C.

These events produced a mighty stir among the Grecian states: and at an assembly of deputies held at Sparta it was resolved to check the Athenian ambition at once. Athens was required to expel the Alcmæonids—a demand levelled at Pericles. She retorted by a similar demand; and after much recrimination Pericles gave his voice for war.

This was the first act of hostility. Three hundred Thebans stole under cover of darkness to Platæa, nearly nine miles off, and were secretly admitted by some of the oligarchic faction. Delaying to begin the expected massacre, they were attacked in the market-place by the townsfolk a little before dawn. Scattering in flight, some escaped, others were killed in the narrow streets and by leaping from the walls, while about one hundred and eighty rushed through an open gate, and found themselves—not outside the wall, as they had expected, but enclosed in a building as in a great trap. And soon afterwards the tidings of a wholesale slaughter filled Greece with horror and alarm. The Thirty Years' Truce was then but fifteen years old.

431 B.C.

Round Sparta were grouped as allies all the Peloponnesian states except Argos and Achaia; round Athens, the chief islands of the Ægean and the towns on the coast of Asia. The Spartans, of Dorian descent, represented aristocracy, and depended upon their military skill; the Athenians, of Ionian blood, fought for democracy, trusting chiefly to the sea.

The plan of Pericles, which was ultimately followed, although the Athenian farmers were reluctant to give up their smiling fields and cosy homesteads to be pillaged, was to concentrate the Attic population in the city, and ravage the coasts of the Peloponnesus with their ships.

The first campaign—431 B.C.—saw Attica invaded by a Peloponnesian army under Archidamus the Spartan King. Advancing to Acharnæ near Athens, they pillaged and wasted, while the prudent hand of Pericles kept back the impatient citizens. They then withdrew. Meanwhile an Athenian fleet attacked the town of Methone in Messenia, which was saved by the prompt valour of young Brasidas the Spartan. In the following autumn Pericles led an Athenian army into Megaris.

The second invasion of Attica—the ravages of a plague which desolated that territory—and the surrender of Potidæa, were the chief events of the second campaign, 430 B.C.

In the spring of 429 B.C. the Spartans under Archidamus began to besiege Platæa by piling timbers from Cithæron round the town, and heaping clay and stones between the layers. The citizens built a brick wall in opposition within a wooden frame, on which raw hides were stretched to keep off the blazing arrows. In vain they dug into the sides and below the foundation of the mound. It continued to rise: and their only plan of meeting it was to erect an inner wall. The Spartan engines, placed upon the mound, threatened the wall; but the besieged caught them with nooses of rope, or threw slung beams upon them, to turn aside or blunt their force. Tired of unavailing efforts, the besiegers then made arrangements for a blockade.

The success of the Athenian admiral Phormio in the Corinthian Gulf also signalized the third year of the war. Meeting a fleet of forty-seven ships with only twenty, he took advantage of a wind, which drove them into confusion, to fall upon the disordered mass. And again, when the Athenian galleys, taken at a disadvantage, were flying before the Peloponnesians, the balance of battle was suddenly turned by a single act of daring. The captain of an Athenian ship, hotly chased by one of the enemy, wheeled his vessel nimbly round an anchored merchantman, and plunged the prow of his galley with destructive force into the side of his pursuer, which filled and sank. The Peloponnesians stopped at once their battle-hymn and their advance. The Athenians promptly improved the chance, and captured six ships.

The death of Pericles, already narrated, left vacant a place as popular leader, which was filled by Cleon, originally a tanner, and a man noisy, boastful, and brazen.

In 428 B.C. Mitylene, the chief city in the important island of Lesbos, revolting against Athens, sought aid from Sparta. This aid was granted. The Athenians, having received timely notice of the intended rising, sent a squadron to Lesbos; and the city of Mitylene was soon doubly enclosed, first by a blockade of ships on the sea side, and afterwards by a wall on the land side.

The siege of Platæa was proceeding meanwhile. A daring movement, by which two hundred and nineteen of the besieged escaped, deserves notice from its picturesque and striking details. Counting the bricks in the encircling wall raised by the besiegers, these brave men made ladders of a suitable height. The wall they aimed at crossing was hollow, and had towers at certain intervals. Choosing a dark night, when howling wind and lashing rain had driven the sentinels under shelter in the cavities of the wall, two hundred and twenty Platæans stole from the city, moving a little apart from each other that their arms might not rattle, and having their right feet bare to secure them from slipping in the mud of the ditch. They climbed the face of the wall in small detachments, the first having only daggers and cuirasses, the next javelins, and the third shields. The noise of a falling brick, detached by some incautious foot, alarmed the guards of the wall; but just at that moment an assault on another part of the rampart drew their attention to its defence. Lights were kindled as signals of alarm; but the townspeople also lit fires, by which the meaning of the flames was lost. In the midst of all, the adventurous Platæans continued to scramble through or over the outer ditch, which was thinly coated with ice, and, when three hundred of the besiegers came running up at last with torches in their hands to the place of danger, those who were waiting on the outer brink, being safely ambushed in the darkness, and aided by the tell-tale lights, sent fatal arrows amongst them that struck down many of the torch-bearers. Running for a while along the road to Thebes, the two hundred and twenty, all but one archer taken at the outer ditch, turned sharply off towards Athens, leaving the twinkling flames of the pursuing torches to stream away in a totally wrong direction.

The year 427 B.C. witnessed the surrender of Mitylene to the Athenians and of Platæa to the Spartans. Barbarous cruelty was displayed by the victors on both occasions. There was indeed an attempt made to countermand the bloody Athenian decree by sending a galley, whose crew rowed night and day, eating morsels of bread dipped in wine or oil, and snatching a little sleep by turns. The countermand arrived just as the decree was about to be read; but much blood was shed nevertheless. In Corcyra also there occurred a brutal massacre of the oligarchic faction, perpetrated by the mob.

In the seventh year of the war (425 B.C.), while an Athenian fleet was sailing to Sicily, Demosthenes proposed to fortify the harbour of Pylos on the western coast of Messenia. A storm having driven the fleet into that place for a time, the soldiers amused themselves by building a wall, carrying the clay on their backs with hands clasped below it. The fleet then sailed away, leaving five ships behind with Demosthenes. In a short time a Spartan fleet came to blockade these; but Demosthenes managed to send two of his five vessels off to recall the Athenian fleet.

A wooded island, called Sphacteria, blocked up the entrance of the harbour, leaving two narrow channels on each side. Landing a force of four hundred and twenty heavy-armed troops on this island, the Spartans drew a chain of galleys across each strait for the purpose of shutting in the Athenians. Demosthenes, enclosing his three ships on the beach with a stockade, went down to the edge of the sea with his few soldiers. The Spartan ships rowed past in small squadrons, but with ceaseless activity, doing but little after all. Brasidas, shouting that it was a shame to prefer a few timber planks to the glory of their country, desired his steersman to run his galley on the shore; but, as he stood on the ladder, ready to spring ashore, several arrows struck him, and he fell back fainting into the ship, while his shield dropped into the sea. Demosthenes hung this on the trophy he erected.

Eurymedon then arrived with the Athenian fleet; and, sailing into both straits, the Athenian ships fell upon the enemy and captured five. So great was the surprise to the Spartans, that some of their ships were dragged empty from the beach, and were only saved by the hands of sailors who waded in and held them tight.

The Spartans then thought fit to request leave to send an embassy to Athens; and begged a truce for the purpose. It was granted on certain conditions, of which the chief was that all the Spartan ships should be given up to the Athenians until the return of the ambassadors. This embassy was unsuccessful owing to the opposition of Cleon. When the truce was ended, the Athenians upon some frivolous pretexts refused to restore the Spartan ships.

But the Athenians now began to find themselves cramped

for room and straitened in their supplies of water; and they were tired keeping watch upon an island, into which food was carried constantly by ships and swimmers, when the wind blew hard. Cleon still blustered at home; and, when it was proposed to send out persons to ascertain the true state of matters, he shot a disdainful glance at Nicias, saying that, if the generals were men, the island would soon be taken, and that, if *he* were in command, he would easily reduce it. Nicias took him sharply at his word by offering to supply troops for the enterprise. Cleon at first tried to back out, but in vain; and then putting a bold face on, he asked for a certain number of troops, and boasted that in twenty days he would either slay the Spartans or bring them captive to Athens. "Thus," thought certain of the wiser sort, "we shall either get the Spartans or lose Cleon—an agreeable result either way."

Strange to say, the tanner, who chose Demosthenes as his colleague, succeeded in making good his boast. Pouring all the troops he had upon the island at night, he forced the garrison to surrender with the loss of nearly one-third of their number. The very cream of Spartan society were among the captives, whom he brought in triumph into the Piræus.

The aristocratic exiles of Corcyra, having fallen into the hands of the Athenians, were placed by them in a certain islet. Some false friends came, and induced the exiles to attempt an escape. Taken in the act, they were handed over to the people of their own island. Stringing them together in twenties, the Corcyreans made the unhappy wretches pass between two files of armed men; and, as each recognized a personal foe, he stuck a dagger in him. Those within the place of confinement then refused to come out. The mob took off the roof and shot arrows at them, as they crouched below. Suicide was then the resource of the exiles. Piercing themselves with arrows or strangling themselves with strips of their rended garments, they escaped murder by taking their own lives. This butchery destroyed the aristocratic faction of Corcyra.

After an unsuccessful attempt on Megara, the Athenians planned a double invasion of Bœotia; Demosthenes being

sent with forty ships to the Corinthian Gulf, while Hippocrates was to enter with an army at Tanagra. Demosthenes found his point of attack too well guarded; and Hippocrates was late in setting out. The latter, reaching Delium on the shore, surrounded it with a wooden palisade; and, having left a garrison there, was on the point of setting out for home, when a Bœotian army came up and offered
424 B.C. battle. The Bœotians, crossing the ridge of the hill that intervened, raised their battle-song, while the Athenians ran to meet them rushing down. A close and bloody fight ensued. The Athenians on the right wing were victorious; but the Thebans broke their left; and, when a body of horsemen appeared upon the height, the Athenians, taking them, as the English mistook the sutlers at Bannockburn, for the van of a new army, gave way and fled. The cause of their terror consisted of a small cavalry force, sent round the back of the hill to fall upon their flank. Seventeen days after the battle the fort of Delium was taken by means of a novel kind of engine. Hollowing two long beams of timber, the Bœotians placed them together to form a tube; and with a pot of lighted combustibles at one end, and a huge pair of bellows at the other, they rolled it on waggons to the barricade. Then, blowing through the tube, they kindled so fierce a flame in the pot, which was pressed against the planks, that these caught fire and drove back the defenders of the rampart. The Athenians, with difficulty and much loss, escaped to their ships.

The famous Spartan general Brasidas had meanwhile been making his way northward to Thrace and Macedonia. He made a conquest of Amphipolis upon the River Strymon, and gained the ascendency over most of the towns studding the three prong-like peninsulas that jut from Chalcidice. Taking advantage of the rage kindled among the Athenian people by these doings, Cleon got himself elected a general of the year, and sailed to the northern shore of the Ægean Sea with thirty galleys, twelve hundred heavy-armed infantry, and three hundred horse, besides a large force of islanders.

His first achievement was the surprise and capture of Torone on the peninsula of Sithonia. He then took post at Eion, a port just where the Strymon enters the sea, and devoted all his energies to gathering a force of allies large enough to overwhelm Brasidas, who was at Amphipolis. The Athenian troops, having little confidence in Cleon, at whom they had been accustomed to jeer and laugh in the theatres, when Aristophanes the comic poet introduced his character on the stage, began to murmur so loudly at his delay that he led them at once to Amphipolis. They advanced to the hill above the city, surprised at seeing no hostile movement to meet them, but little aware that sharp Spartan eyes were watching them from an eminence across the river. Cleon, vapouring about his sorrow that he had brought no scaling-ladders to climb the walls, went on to view the lake above the city; but Brasidas came down into the city and prepared for an attack upon the foolhardy foe. When Cleon came back, he saw that a retreat was necessary, and ordered his men to move. So little common sense had he, and so ignorant did he prove to be of the simplest principles of soldiership, that he turned towards the foe that side of his men which had no shield to guard it. The consequences were instant and fatal. From the nearest gates of Amphipolis, flung suddenly open, streams of men came charging in double-quick time up the hill. The centre was driven in; the right wing broken. Brasidas however fell with a mortal wound; and the hurled spear of a targeteer brought fugitive Cleon to the ground, and stopped his blustering for ever. Only seven men were slain on the Spartan side, while six hundred of the Athenian force perished.

There was then a pause in the warfare, and a distinct leaning towards peace. Athens had suffered in Bœotia, and her allies were troubled with an epidemic of revolt; Sparta had also felt the scourge of war, and dreaded the rising of her helots, while the flower of her manhood, taken at Sphacteria, still languished in captivity. Accordingly King Pleistoanax in Sparta, and the cautious Nicias at Athens concurred in recommending the peace, which bears in history the name of the latter. It was a peace for fifty years. 421 B.C.

We now see rising to prominence in the story of Greece two of her greatest names.

Alcibiades, the son of Clinias and Dinomache, was by both father and mother of the noblest Athenian blood. Becoming the ward of Pericles, he entered at the age of eighteen upon the enjoyment of a vast fortune. From early childhood he had been of striking beauty, which only bloomed the brighter as he advanced from youth to manhood. Self-willed and resolute, he bent both playmates and tutors to his purposes. A lisp in his utterance and a certain affectation in his manner of walking gave piquancy to his speech and his general appearance. He strikes the reader of Grecian history as a spoiled boy on a magnificent scale. There was something of the inflated heroic about him, when as a boy he flung himself before a loaded waggon, that threatened to disturb his game of dice, and bade the carter then drive on, if he liked. And in his refusal to learn the flute, because the practice contorted the face and prevented the musician from speaking, we can see wilfulness with a dash of common sense beneath it. Such was the famous Alcibiades at the outset of his life.

Older by about twenty years and of widely different parentage was Socrates, the son of Sophroniscus the sculptor and Phænarete the midwife. The ugly face of this thick-lipped flat-nosed man did not repel the friendship of Alcibiades, who singled him out from the crowd of his dependents, and made him his most intimate companion, his "guide, philosopher, and friend." Mutual acts of service formed another bond between the pair, when Socrates carried the wounded Alcibiades to a place of safety at the siege of Potidæa, and Alcibiades had the pleasure of returning the kindness at Delium. But the great founder of the Attic philosophy could not keep this handsome profligate within the bounds of order and propriety. It was the custom of the young Athenians to breed quails for fighting; and one day Alcibiades in a public assembly of the people was so much delighted with their applause that he allowed the bird he carried beneath his robe to fly away. All public business was forgotten in the race to catch the quail. His imperious temper may be judged from the fact that he imprisoned a famous painter in his house for months in order to have certain decorations completed; and his wantonness from the fact that he gave his father-in-law a box on the ear, simply because some silly companion had dared him to commit the act. At the Olympic games he won three crowns and outshone all by the splendour of the feasts he gave.

This splendid prodigal, restless under the peace of Nicias, in the making of which he had been overlooked as too young for such negotiations, sought means of plunging his country once more into the war from which she had just emerged. The people of Argos, being then engaged in discussing the terms of a Spartan alliance, received from him a secret message that Athens was inclined to make a treaty with them: and they accordingly broke off negotiations with their southern neighbours and closed with the Athenians.

In a direct line between Argos and the island of Ægina, whence there was easy communication with Athens, lay a strip of coast called Epidaurus, on which the Argives now cast covetous eyes as affording them access to their new ally. Upon a religious pretext they accordingly invaded this territory, to the aid of which a Spartan force advanced. The Athenians then sent Alcibiades with a thousand men to support the invaders. After some delay the Spartan army under Agis marched into Argolis; but a truce was made for four months. This displeased both the Argives, who pelted the general that had proposed the measure, and the Spartans, who threatened to pull down the house of Agis. Alcibiades, persuading the Argives that the truce was void as being made without the consent of their allies, induced them to assail Orchomenos in Arcadia, which yielded. This broke the peace, and the Peloponnesian war was resumed.

Agis, being in disgrace, had difficulty in retaining the command of the Spartan army; a council of ten, without whose sanction he could not give battle, was appointed to control his movements. But he soon recovered his fame as a military leader.

Finding the foe in a strong position near Mantinea, he enticed them from their steep stronghold into the plain by proceeding to turn some disputed rivers in the Tegean plain

so as to overflow the lands of Mantinea. Ignorant whereabout the foe lay, the Argives and Athenians were
418 B.C. moving on the lower ground, when Agis caught sight of them rounding the shoulder of a hill. Though startled at first, the Spartans fell into rank quietly and steadily, and marched to battle to the sound of their flutes, whose sweet music accorded well with the pealing notes of the national war-songs. The Spartan lines crowded too much to the right, owing to that tendency among all ancient troops to press the side unguarded by a shield against the next man; but in spite of this weakening of the left wing, and the consequent effect upon the centre, from which men were detached to support it, Agis gained a splendid victory, which restored the reputation of Sparta as a great military state.

Argos then formed an alliance with Sparta; but the democratic faction, reviving in the place, endeavoured to establish their power by building long walls from the city to its harbour. These however were destroyed by Agis, before they were finished.

Alcibiades induced the Athenians to demand submission from the island of Melos, which evidently had Spartan leanings; and, when the high-spirited inhabitants refused to accede, a blockade began, which lasted some months, and ended, to the lasting disgrace of Athens, in the massacre of all the males, and the slavery of the women and children.

The Sicilian Expedition.—Sicily had long been an object of covetous regard to the Athenians. Foremost among those who advocated a naval expedition thither, was Alcibiades, who, widening his schemes even to Libya and Carthage, contrived to raise such a breeze of talk among the young men that some of them used to sit all day in the gymnasium tracing the outlines of these places on the sand. Three generals—Nicias, Alcibiades, and Lamachus—being appointed to command an armament, preparations were made for setting out. In the midst of these an event happened, which completely changed the current of Alcibiades' life. One night all the statues of Mercury in the city—and such a bust stood at every door—were chipped and mutilated by persons unknown. Rightly or wrongly Alcibiades was charged with this impiety; and there was superadded an accusation of having mimicked certain sacred mysteries at a drunken revel in his house. He sought an immediate hearing, but he had foes powerful enough to cause the postponement of a public trial for an uncertain time.

Then, with trumpet-sound and prayers, libations from golden cups and the triumphal music of the pæan, a splendidly equipped armament left the Piræus, bound for Sicily. When the full number had assembled at Corcyra, this Armada of the ancient seas contained one hundred and thirty-four galleys of the first class; and on board were five thousand heavy infantry and more than a thousand archers and slingers. A mistake was committed in sending only thirty horse.

415 B.C.

There was much distrust among the Italian-Greeks, when the fleet arrived off Rhegium; and the leaders were divided in opinion as to the operations that should be undertaken. The counsel of Alcibiades prevailed; and Catana was surprised. Just then however the Salaminian galley, used by the Athenians for state purposes, arrived to bring Alcibiades home in order to stand his trial. Pretending to yield himself up, he went on board his own galley, and accompanied the *Salaminia* to Thurii. There he went ashore and hid himself, until the ship had sailed. Great was the rage of the Athenians at his escape; and deep were the curses of the priesthood, as they waved their red banners towards the east, condemning him to death and infamy. "I will show them I am still alive," were the threatening words of the exile, when he heard of the doom that had been pronounced. From Thurii he went to Argos: from Argos to Sparta, where he adopted all the customs of the place, which mightily pleased the people. Instead of the purple robe, the golden shield, the perfumed bath, the delicate supper, to which he had been used, he took with apparent relish to the black broth, the coarse garb, the cold plunge, to which the disciples of Lycurgus were compelled to inure themselves.

The siege of Syracuse was the great event of the Sicilian expedition. The slow and cautious Nicias undertook certain expeditions, which did little more than display his timidity; nor was it until autumn that he approached Syracuse.

Having no cavalry, he invented a plan, by which he gained a landing there unopposed. A native of Catana came to Syracuse, as if friendly to that city, and, saying that the Athenians were in the habit of deserting their camp every night to sleep in the town, urged the Syracusans to fling all their force some night on the camp. They took the bait, and marched in full array to Catana; while the Athenians, hastening by sea to the unguarded city, established themselves under the height Olympeium, rising on the inner shore of the Great Harbour near the mouth of the Anapus. To secure their position, the invaders broke down the bridge over that river. There was soon a skirmish, in which the Athenians had the advantage, the Sicilians being frightened by a thunder-storm.

When the Athenians went away to winter at Naxos, the people of Syracuse sought aid in Greece, where their cause was warmly espoused by Corinth and Sparta. Alcibiades, now a denizen of the latter state, urged their claims strongly, showing how this siege of Syracuse was meant to be only the prelude to conquests, which were to include Carthage, Italy, and all Greece. Accordingly the skilful Spartan general Gylippus was appointed to the command of a Sicilian expedition.

The Athenians devoted part of the winter to collecting corn, money, horses, bricks, and iron in Sicily and elsewhere; and in the spring managed to occupy Epipolæ, a ridge behind the town, on the very day that seven hundred of the Syracusan force had been desired to secure the position.

Since Syracuse was built on a rounded promontory, to which an island had been joined, the Athenian plan was to build from sea to sea a wall of crescent shape, whose concave should enclose the town. As soon as the besieged saw these works commence, they began to erect cross-walls to break the line of circumvallation; and so urgent was the need that even the wood of the sacred olive groves was unsparingly devoted to this use. The Athenians resisted this counterworking fiercely, laying boards across the mud of the river-marsh in order to get at the Syracusan soldiers. In one of the engagements Lamachus was killed, but the attempts of the besieged were for a time completely baffled; and Nicias was in high hopes that for him was reserved the termination of a successful war.

But soon Gylippus, having landed at Himera and collected men in Sicily, marched upon Syracuse with about three thousand troops. Permitted by the negligence of Nicias, he ascended Epipolæ, and then began to aid the Syracusans in making a wall, which should cross Epipolæ and open communication with the interior. This work was afterwards successfully accomplished. Nicias now shifted ground, occupying with part of his forces the southern headland called Plemyrium, on which he built three forts. He then sent home a letter, describing the wretched condition of his ships and men, and praying that a successor might be appointed to relieve him, for he was broken by disease.

Though a Peloponnesian garrison had occupied Decelea, a rocky height fifteen miles from Athens, near the source of the Cephisus, and were ravaging ceaselessly from this centre, and though the city was crowded and in want, it was decreed by the Athenians to send aid to Nicias in Sicily; and Demosthenes and Eurymedon were appointed to lead an armament thither.

Meanwhile Gylippus, during a sea-fight in the Great Harbour, took the forts on the Plemyrium; and, although the Athenians were victorious for a while in the naval engagement, they were nevertheless blockaded in the enclosure where they had fought. The Syracusans commenced then to enclose their triremes by a palisade of stakes fixed in the bottom of the harbour; and the Athenians laboured hard to prevent them, by sawing the piles below water and then breaking them with ropes. What with driving and diving, sawing and hauling, the harbour was in a continual ferment. These stakes tore many a plank from the sides of the Athenian triremes, before they were sawn asunder by the divers.

While Gylippus attacked the wall, the Syracusans, who had strengthened and made broad the prows of their galleys with planks of timber, made a movement against the Athenian triremes. Nicias had provided a nook of refuge for his ships by mooring a line of merchantmen, through which the enemy feared to pass, lest leaden dolphins, hanging on the masts, might drop and sink them. Within this fence the Athenian ships retired, after some days' fighting had resulted to the advantage of the Syracusans.

The hearts of the besieged died within them, when they saw the harbour beaten into foam by the oars of seventy-three galleys, which bore eight thousand troops under Demosthenes and Eurymedon. But this feeling did not last; for a night-attack on Epipolæ, under the light of a fitful moon, though successful at first, ended in the total rout of the Athenians, whose watchwords were heard by the enemy, and some of whose allies, singing war-songs in the Dorian dialect, were mistaken by them for foes. Many were driven over the crags; and those who escaped in the faint dawn to the plains were cut down by the Syracusan cavalry.

Demosthenes then urged an immediate return home; Nicias with characteristic sluggishness suggested delay; but, when Gylippus, who had been collecting aid throughout the island, re-entered the city with succours, a secret retreat was resolved upon. Just then occurred an eclipse of the moon, which roused the superstitions of the soldiery and of Nicias, whose credulity was great. The soothsayers insisted that it was necessary to delay for twenty-seven days. This proved to be a fatal pause; for the Syracusans and the Spartans made a double attack as before—by land upon the wall, by sea upon the triremes—and, having driven Eurymedon into a corner, destroyed both his ships and himself. The whole Athenian fleet was then in great peril, especially when a blazing fire-ship came drifting down among the galleys; but the efforts of the land troops and the skill of the mariners saved a proportion of the vessels. The Syracusans then shut the mouth of the harbour by anchoring a chain of small ships sideways from shore to shore. Vainly the Athenians grappled the ships with iron claws and strove to tear a gap; the Sicilians chased them to the inner shore.

There was then no resource but a land march, and even in this the evil fortune of the Athenians pursued them. Hermocrates, who had been the leader of the Syracusans throughout the whole affair, advised that all the passes should be seized. The Syracusans were too busy with the feast of Hercules to do so on that day; a secret messenger was therefore sent to Nicias, warning him not to leave that night, as all the roads were occupied. Believing this to have come from a friend, he waited a day; and then the two divisions marched out to their own destruction through a country thorny with hostile spears. Leaving the dead and the sick behind, the Athenians pressed up the Anapus in a hollow square, harassed at every step by flying squadrons of horse. After a futile effort at escape by leaving their watch-fires blazing and turning sharply at an angle towards the sea, the division of Demosthenes found themselves hemmed in among olive gardens, and were forced to surrender. The troops of Nicias, somewhat in advance, surrendered a little later at the river Assinarus, which was filled with men, whose scorching thirst compelled them to drink water mingled with the blood of their dead comrades.

413 B.C.

Nicias and Demosthenes suffered death. Seven thousand inferior men lived, or died, as the case might be, on barley-meal and water for seventy days in the quarries of Epipolæ, before they were sold into slavery. It is stated that such of the prisoners as could recite verses from the plays of Euripides received kinder treatment in return for the delight their elocution afforded to their masters.

There are two stories about the reception of this dreadful news in Athens. One states that it was first brought by a foreigner, who, landing at Piræus, went into a barber's shop and announced it as matter of common talk elsewhere. The poor barber, running to the Archons, found himself stretched upon the rack as payment for his trouble. The other describes the Athenian people as gathered in the theatre, when the sad tidings spread from bench to bench, without however exciting any visible emotion among the audience, for the groans of every Athenian heart were smothered in the presence of the strangers who were there.

Then the allies of Athens began to revolt, and claim the protection of the Spartans, who made an alliance also with Persia. Alcibiades got deep into the favour of Tissaphernes, the Persian satrap, in hopes, no doubt, like the unjust steward, of providing for himself a refuge in the day of trouble.

A naval war then began on the coast of Asia. Violent

efforts were put forth by the Athenians to retake Chios. Their centre of operations was fixed at Samos.

Alcibiades, who desired restoration, sent Pisander to Athens on this business; and his envoy, becoming associated with Phrynicus and Antiphon, brought about an oligarchic revolution, which placed the power really in the hands of the Four Hundred, and nominally in those of a larger council of Five Thousand. One of the earliest movements of the former body was to proceed, each with a dagger peeping from below his robe, to the public hall and expel the old council of Five Hundred.

But the spirit of the fleet and army at Samos was democratic. With one voice both mariners and soldiers called upon Alcibiades to lead them to the Piræus; but he had the good sense rather to restrain them. Athens meanwhile was much disturbed. The oligarchic faction, being in **411 B.C.** the ascendant, fortified a mole at the mouth of the harbour, where all the corn was piled in a public granary; but the tide soon turned. These works were pulled down; Phrynicus, one of the oligarchic leaders, was killed in the street at mid-day; and Theramenes became the chief of the democratic party.

One day there came a cry from the harbour that a Peloponnesian fleet was near Salamis. It proved to be true; but the ships, instead of attacking the Piræus, sailed up the Euripus, and between Eretria and Oropus met an Athenian squadron, which was beaten with the loss of twenty-two ships.

The revolt of Eubœa then fell like a thunder-bolt on the Athenians, stirring them to so great a pitch of excitement that a public assembly in the Pnyx deposed the Four Hundred, and committed all power to the Five Thousand.

The hopes of the Athenians were revived by a naval victory they won over the Peloponnesians at Cynossema in the Hellespont. The recall of Alcibiades, which had been mooted at Athens, was delayed for a time by the craft of Tissaphernes, who arrested the exile when he came with presents in his hand. But Alcibiades escaped in a month, and, **410 B.C.** rejoining the Athenian fleet, sailed under cover of a thick fog to Cyzicus in the Propontis, where he contrived to get between the Peloponnesian fleet and their harbour. Great was their consternation, when the sunbeams rent the curtain of the mist and disclosed the galleys of Alcibiades. Hastily ceasing from the mimicry of warfare, in which they had been engaged for the sake of drill and exercise, they pushed their ships on the nearest shore, and fought from deck. In vain. They lost their whole fleet.

After this blow Sparta proposed peace; but it was refused by the democratic party in Athens.

During the year 408 B.C. the war centred in the Bosporus, where by the skill and prowess of Alcibiades the Athenians became masters of Byzantium.

There was then nothing to delay the return of Alcibiades to his native place. With bulwarks all hung with captured shields, and masts fluttering with captured flags of many hues, he entered the harbour; but he did not venture to land until he saw friendly faces in the crowd on shore. An ovation awaited him on his landing; tears were shed; garlands showered on him; and old men pointed out to the young the hero, who had restored the national honour so tarnished in the Sicilian disasters. In the Assembly a golden
crown was placed upon his head, and he was made 407
absolute commander of all the Athenian forces. B.C.
The excitement grew into a frenzy of admiration, when, under the very eyes of the Spartans on Decelea, he escorted safely to Eleusis those charged with the celebration of the famous Mysteries, which had been shorn of their most striking ceremonies owing to the presence of the enemy near the Sacred Way.

But the triumph of Alcibiades was short-lived. The Spartans selected as the fittest general to oppose him the half-blood Lysander, whose mother's humble origin deprived her son of certain privileges due to his father's rank. Sailing to Ephesus, he measured his strength with the Athenians in the battle of Notium. Having occasion to go elsewhere, Alcibiades left the fleet in charge of Antiochus, the skipper of his own trireme, with strict orders not to fight under any provocation. But this man, overrating his own seamanship, sailed in his galley into the harbour of Ephesus, to abuse the Spartans and taunt them with cowardice. They gave chase;

other Athenians came up; and a battle ensued, in which the scattered groups of Athenian galleys were ploughed to pieces by the darting prows of the Spartan vessels.

The enemies of Alcibiades—and he had not a few at Athens—turned this loss into the means of his deposal, upon which he retired to the Chersonese; and Conon, associated with nine colleagues, became Athenian commander at Samos.

There was also a change on the Spartan side, upon which Callicratidas, a man most eager for fight, came into office as admiral. Chasing Conon into the harbour of Mitylene, he blocked him up there. But Conon managed, by sending two swift galleys out to sea, while the Spartans were lazily enjoying their mid-day meal, to convey news of his difficulty to Athens. A great mustering of ships began; and soon, on the islets of Arginusæ off the Æolian shore, twinkling lights announced the encampment of an Athenian force. The numbers of the opposing fleets were one hundred and fifty on the Athenian side, against one hundred and twenty Spartan ships. In the battle that ensued the Athenians were victorious, but with the heavy loss of twenty-five galleys, which were destroyed so far out at sea as to cause the death of a large proportion of their crews, whom a storm prevented the other Athenian galleys from assisting.

406 B.C.

But here a great wrong was done. By the wicked schemes of a naval officer called Theramenes, the eight generals, who should have received thanks and rewards, were condemned to death, by a vote of the Athenian Assembly, for not assisting their comrades; and six, who had gone home after the battle, were executed. A city, which could be bent to commit a criminal blunder so huge, could not expect to live long in freedom.

Retribution, swift and complete, came next year at Ægospotami in the strait of the Hellespont, whither the Athenian fleet had followed Lysander and his ships. For five days the Athenians offered battle, and grew every day more careless, when they found their challenge declined. Beaching their galleys on the sand, they straggled to the villages in search of food. They were watched by eyes both hostile and friendly. Lysander sent

405 B.C.

swift galleys after them every day; and Alcibiades looked from the towers of his castle on the Chersonese and saw the madness of their conduct. The latter ventured to point out to the Athenian generals their mistake, but he was dismissed with insulting words. On the fifth day Lysander's spy-galleys hoisted a shield, when they saw the Athenians out of their ships—and then down, like a cloud of sharp-beaked falcons, darted the waiting squadrons of the Spartans. The victory was easy; for empty ships lay slanting on the sand; and their crews were scattered for miles around. Conon escaped to Cyprus with eight ships: and the *Paralus* rushed across the sea to Athens with the fatal news.

But one event remained to complete the humiliation of the city of Pericles. Pausanias with a land-force encamped among the trees of the Academy, while Lysander blocked up the mouth of the Piræus with a chain of one hundred and fifty galleys. Within the city, to which in the darkness of one terrible night the *Paralus* had come, wringing a bitter cry from streets crowded with sleepless citizens, there was the suicidal tumult of faction, and soon the gnawing anguish of hunger, for the city was crowded with fugitives, for whom no food had been provided. The end of all was surrender, ignominious and complete: Athens no longer possessed either ships or walls.

404 B.C.

While Lysander the Spartan proceeded, with the music of flutes and the glitter of garlands, to destroy the walls of the captured city, Theramenes procured the appointment of thirty magistrates, known to history as the Thirty Tyrants. Their chief duty was to draw up a new code of laws. They adopted at once a cruel policy; and, dissensions having sprung up among them, Theramenes was impeached and obliged to drink the fatal juice of hemlock. The Thirty then grew bloodier and more rapacious still; and all Attica groaned under their oppression. Relief came in the person of Thrasybulus, an exile at Thebes, who seized the mountain fort of Phyle, defeated the skirmishers sent to attack him, made himself master of Piræus, and overthrew the army of the Tyrants in the battle of

403 B.C.

Munychia, fought at the foot of the jutting headland of that name. The Thirty being deposed, authority at Athens was vested in a Council of Ten.

Meanwhile Alcibiades, who had escaped into Asia after the battle of Ægos-potami, met a violent death. While sleeping in a Phrygian village, the house he lodged in was set on fire, and, when he ran out, a shower of missiles from a ring of men struck him to the earth with mortal wounds. The murder is thought to have been the deed of Pharnabazus, the Persian satrap.

A few years brought a yet greater man to a more memorable death. The name of Socrates has already been associated with that of Alcibiades. A brave soldier in front of the foe—an incorruptible and dauntless senator—a teacher who sought no reward but the approval of good men and the love of his disciples—this illustrious Athenian nevertheless incurred, by his very purity of aim and the deep insight of his genius, the envy of some leading men of his day. Aristophanes attacked him in the comedy of *The Clouds;* the accomplished but savage Critias—most brilliant of the Thirty Tyrants—persecuted him incessantly. And at length, upon the restoration of democracy, his personal foes set on foot against him an impeachment, containing three charges:—(1) of not believing in the established gods of the state: (2) of introducing new deities: (3) of corrupting the young. He met these charges with a careless courage; and, when the verdict went against him, named a trifling fine as the proper punishment for his offences. But his enemies were in terrible earnest, and sentence of death was pronounced by a majority of eighty votes. The Sacred Ship, with Apollo's laurel-crown upon its stern, was then on the point of starting for Delos, and no criminal's death could stain the city until its return. There was accordingly a pause of thirty days, which Socrates spent chiefly in conversation with chosen friends, whose kindly suggestions at escape he put mildly but firmly aside. Then, drinking the cup of hemlock, he lay down, and died in his seventieth year.

399 B.C.

CHAPTER III.

THE TEN THOUSAND.

Design of Cyrus. His Greek Force. Across Euphrates. | The Cloud of Dust. Death of Cyrus. Greek Officers Seized. | Xenophon. Thalatta, Thalatta. Xenophon at Scillus.

CYRUS, the second son of Darius, King of Persia, formed the design of ousting Artaxerxes Mnemon, his elder brother, from the throne. In this scheme he was encouraged by his mother Parysatis. His enemy Tissaphernes charged him on one occasion with a plan to murder Artaxerxes, who would have put him to death but for the loud and piteous clamours of the Queen-mother. In spite of his brother's clemency Cyrus continued to nourish his designs. And, when his preparations were complete, he set out from Sardis in the spring of 401 B.C. with a force considerably over one hundred thousand men. But the part of this army, upon which he depended most, was a body of Greeks, chiefly from the Asiatic cities, ultimately amounting to thirteen thousand, under the command of Clearchus, a Spartan exile. In the fortunes of these Greeks the interest of the expedition centres.

401 B.C.

At a town in Phrygia Cyrus reviewed his army for the amusement of the Queen of Cilicia, who had supplied him with money; and in the course of the manœuvres he gave orders for the Greeks to make a mimic charge. So terrible was the advance of the serried phalanx, as the warriors, flashing with brass and glowing with scarlet, came on with thundering tread and pealing shouts, that the barbarians fled in dismay, and the Queen jumped from her car and ran with the trembling rout, while a great roar of laughter went up from the Grecian ranks. Cyrus, with a quiet smile, thought how well such an incident would further his cause, when he met the forces of Artaxerxes.

At Tarsus the Greeks, seeing clearly that Pisidia was not,

as had been announced, the object of the expedition, began to suspect its real meaning, and at first refused to proceed. Clearchus, not without some personal danger from hurled stones, at last persuaded them to go on. They passed from Cilicia into Syria by the mountain-passes just at the angle of the sea; and then advanced towards the Euphrates. Ever since the renewal of their march they had been learning to see more clearly whither they were going; but the promise of money at Babylon still lured them on.

At Thapsacus, where they crossed the Euphrates, they found the ferry-boats burned; but the stream proved to be only breast-high, and they waded through. Hunger, thirst discords, quagmires, treachery, all impeded, but did not stop the march towards Babylon. Orontes, who had already twice received the pardon of Cyrus for acts of revolt, was intercepted while planning desertion, and was put to death.

After a midnight review Cyrus, who had promised every Greek a golden crown, looked eagerly for the foe, whom tidings had led him to expect. They did not come. He passed a trench, evidently dug for defence but now unguarded; and, in the belief that there would be no battle, he grew somewhat careless in his line of march. But, when one day at noon his jaded soldiers came near the village of Cunaxa, about sixty miles from Babylon, a horseman rode through the ranks on a steed all white with foam, crying out that the army of the King was coming in full battle array. Presently a great cloud of dust, sometimes broken by gleams of metallic light, arose on the horizon. There were nine hundred thousand men of all arms in the host; and one hundred and fifty scythed cars. So unequal were the numbers that the left wing of Cyrus' army did not reach the centre of the enemy's line. The order of Cyrus to the Greeks was to attack the main body, where his brother commanded in person.

The Greeks began to sing the pæan, and, quickening their pace, raised the battle-cry, and struck spear and shield together as they ran. Opening to let the chariots pass, they then rushed upon the barbarians, who had no courage to await their onset. Cyrus was delighted, and dashed with a handful of men upon the six thousand round the King. It was a brief and unequal combat. With the words, "I see the man," he rode at Artaxerxes, and struck him wounded from his horse; but a javelin, whizzing from some hand unknown, hit Cyrus in the head, and left him an easy victim to the blades of the surrounding foes.

The victorious Greeks were soon visited by heralds from the Persian King, who demanded their arms. These they would not yield; and so much was the monarch impressed with their valour, that he sent Tissaphernes to negotiate a peace with them. The terms which they accepted were, "that they should have a safe-conduct to their own country, and a market on the road; and that wherever none was furnished they should be allowed to take necessaries; that on their part they should engage to do no mischief to the King's territories."

The Greeks then began to move under the guidance and escort of Tissaphernes towards the Tigris, which they crossed. Certain suspicions arose, but the wily Persians lulled them to rest, loading Clearchus with civilities. The crisis came not far from the point, at which a tributary called Zabatus, from the Armenian Mountains, joins the Tigris. Clearchus and four of the Grecian generals, having gone to the quarters of Tissaphernes for the purpose of holding a conference, were arrested, while some subalterns and privates, who had accompanied them, were slain. All the five, except one, were beheaded.

In this emergency a certain volunteer named Xenophon, a pupil and friend of Socrates, dreamed a dream, which led him to spring from his bed and call the officers together. New generals were elected before the day broke; and Xenophon was requested to take the chief command. Burning their tents and carts and keeping only what was absolutely necessary, the army then began to move in a hollow square. Its adventures and misadventures have been clearly and gracefully narrated in the book called *Anabasis*, written by the man who led them. Attacked by Mithridates, whom their want of cavalry and light troops rendered them powerless to pursue, and tormented by a ceaseless rain of arrows from the force of Tissaphernes, they struggled bravely on through Media. When they reached a part of the Tigris, where the water ran deep under precipitous cliffs, they were forced to turn their march into the mountains of Carduchia, which were filled with fleet-footed archers, who could drive a shaft through a breast-plate. And, as they went, tongues of flame sprang up and spread the news from hill to hill. Here Tissaphernes ceased the pursuit; but the Greeks had still to fight their way. At the river Centrites, whose banks were lined with foes, Xenophon had another lucky dream, and soon discovered a ford, by which the army crossed. In Armenia their human foes disappeared for a time; but the snow and the north wind fought sorely against them still.

After forcing their way through hosts of barbarians, the vanguard reached the summit of the ridge Theches (now Kóp Tagh), and with tear-dimmed eyes saw the waters of the Euxine heaving against the northern horizon. From rank to rank, in the various dialects of the Grecian tongue, a joyous cry spread: The Sea! the Sea! and weather-worn warriors fell sobbing on their comrades' necks, as they thought of their escape.

At Trapezus they found themselves among friends. When a review was held at Cerasus, another seaport of the Euxine shore, it was discovered that eight thousand six hundred survived out of the original force of ten thousand. At Cotyora they got ships, which carried them to Sinope and Heraclea; and so, partly by land and partly by sea, they made their way to Chrysopolis, opposite Byzantium.

After some service with the King of Thrace, Xenophon received sentence of banishment from Athens, and joined the Spartans, who gave him an estate near Scillus in Elis, overlooking the Olympian plain. Here he lived in peace for some time among his books and his trees, until he was either driven by an attack to Corinth, where he died, or recalled to his birth-place by a tardy decree.

CHAPTER IV.

STRUGGLE BETWEEN SPARTA AND THEBES.

A VERY distinguished man, named Agesilaus, ascended the throne of Sparta in 399 B.C. He signalized himself immediately afterwards by crushing a plot to overturn the Spartan oligarchy. In company with Lysander, he went to Asia Minor, where Tissaphernes, the Persian satrap, was scheming against the independence of the Greek cities. Owing to a breach between the King and himself, Lysander was sent to the Hellespont; and some years later was slain in an attack upon the town of Haliartus in Bœotia. When Tissaphernes assumed the attitude of war, Agesilaus marched towards Sardis, and there (395 B.C.) defeated an army of Persian horse. The career of victory, thus begun, was continued with brilliant success, until a decree of the Ephors recalled Agesilaus from Asia to Greece.

The emissaries of Persia had by bribery and persuasion caused the formation of a league against Sparta. Thebes, Athens, Corinth, and Argos banded themselves together to check her pride. Under Conon, the Athenian admiral, whose flight from Ægos-potami has been noticed, a fleet, equipped at the expense of the Persians, defeated the Spartan fleet signally off Cnidus, in Caria. Pisander, the Spartan admiral, was killed in the action. This calamity shook the Spartan power; but Agesilaus, meeting an army of the allies on the plain of Coronea in Bœotia, engaged them with such fury as to scatter them in flight. The struggle went on at Corinth and elsewhere. Conon, having obtained a grant of Persian gold sufficient to rebuild the Long Walls and the fortifications of

394 B.C.

Piræus, clad Athens once more in the armour of stone, of which she had been stripped by her triumphant antagonist.

The war, however, was soon closed by the Treaty
387 B.C. of Antalcidas, framed by the clever Spartan whose name it bears. The leading terms of this peace were, that the cities in Asia, and the islands of Clazomenæ and Cyprus, should belong to the King of Persia, while every other Greek city should be free, except Lemnos, Imbros, and Scyros, which were to remain under Athenian rule.

But Sparta had grown too haughty to submit long to the chain of such a treaty. She stretched out her hand against Mantinea, whose citizens she scattered, and she forced Phlius to recall certain exiles at her bidding. And, seeing away in the north the state of Olynthus, strong in natural advantages, and filled with an ambitious people, she resolved to check this rival, before the task might perhaps become too difficult.

Out of the minor war, thus begun, grew a more famous contest. For, while a Spartan army was marching through Bœotia towards Olynthus, the soldiers took possession of the Cadmea or citadel of Thebes. It happened in this way. Phœbidas, the brother of Eudamidas, to whom the conduct of the Olynthian war was intrusted, stopped beside Thebes for a time. Within the city the oligarchic faction still existed under the leadership of Leontiades the polemarch; and this man was so filled with the spirit of faction
382 B.C. that he proposed to put the citadel into the hands of the Spartans. Choosing a festival of Ceres, when the castle was filled with women, and a period of the day when the heat of the meridian sun had driven the citizens within doors, Leontiades followed Phœbidas, who had set his troops in motion as if to resume his march, and led him into the Cadmea. The leader of the popular party, Ismenias, was arrested, upon which about four hundred Thebans fled to Athens.

And then arose two men, whose names shine like stars in Grecian story. As from the furnace comes the purest gold, and from the anvil the strongest iron, so from the troubles of exile and the miseries of civil war grew the genius and the fame of Pelopidas and Epaminondas. The former, rich and noble, not in birth only but by nature too, was one of the fugitives who sought a home in Athens : the latter, a poor philosopher and scholar whom nobody considered likely to interfere in politics, remained quietly at home, waiting for the time when Thebes might need his help.

About three years after this seizure, Pelopidas and a few of the Theban exiles, in pursuance of a plan they had formed, entered Thebes in the dress of peasants. Their chief friends in the city were two—Charon, to whose house they had been invited, and Phyllidas, who had become secretary to some of the polemarchs. A timely snow-shower, driven by a biting wind, cleared the streets so that they reached the house of Charon in safety. The secretary had bidden two of the polemarchs to a feast at his house ; and just as the wine was beginning to circle briskly, word was 379 brought that the exiles were within the gates. B.C. Charon was sent for, and the loud knocking at his door startled the conspirators, who had now exchanged their rustic garb for armour. But Charon, going boldly to the banquet-room, professed ignorance about the men, but promised to make inquiry. An urgent letter from Athens soon afterwards reached the polemarch Archias, detailing the whole plot; but with a drunken smile he said, "Business to-morrow," and pushed it under the pillow on which, after the Grecian fashion, he was reclining. By-and-by there came into the banquet-room Charon and his accomplices, dressed in women's clothes over their armour, and having their faces shadowed with leafy wreaths of vine and poplar. Their swords made short work of the drunken polemarchs. Leontidas, attacked in his bed-room, neglected to put out the lamp, whose light enabled Pelopidas to slay him. Then, sending word to Attica and emptying the cutlers' shops, the exiles waited all night in the streets, which were filled with flitting torches and resounded with noise and terror.

The evacuation of the Cadmea by the Spartan garrison was the necessary result of this surprise, and Thebes was free.

The year 379 B.C. was rendered further notable by the fall of Olynthus before Spartan prowess.

The Theban War then began. At first the Spartans acted

on the offensive by invading Bœotia under Cleombrotus and Agesilaus. The Athenians, being led to side with Thebes, increased their navy, and put it to gallant use by defeating the Spartan fleet off Naxos (376 B.C.). In the following year Pelopidas, chiefly by the aid of three hundred picked men, called the City Band, but thereafter known by the more famous appellation of the Sacred Band, won the battle of Tegyra or Orchomenus by attacking in turn the several divisions of the Spartan army, after its two generals had fallen. This victory made Thebes supreme among the cities of Bœotia.

Athens and Sparta then made peace with each other, and Thebes was left unfriended in the struggle. Such a position however served only to develop the greatness of the men who had become her leaders.

When Cleombrotus the Spartan led a force of ten thousand foot and one thousand horse into the Bœotian territory, the Thebans, to the number of six thousand, met him at the little town of Leuctra; and there, on ground cursed by an ancient Sparta crime, was fought a battle which ranks among the greatest in the annals of warfare. At first there was some hesitation among the other Theban generals; but Epaminondas, one of the Bœotarchs, and Pelopidas, Captain of the Sacred Band, gave their voice for immediate action. The omens, to which ancient Greeks trusted much, were favourable to the Thebans, but adverse to Sparta. The Theban victory seems to have been due to the admirable tactics of Epaminondas, seconded by the prompt courage of his friend. Drawing up his phalanx fifty deep in the shape of a wedge, the former cut off the right wing of the Spartan army from the main body, and the Sacred Band, charging the confused mass, broke and routed it. Cleombrotus fell with a mortal wound, and the rest of the Peloponnesian army then fled to their intrenched camp.

371 B.C.

For Spartan invasions of Bœotia we now begin to find Theban invasions of the Peloponnesus. Aided by many allies, among whom Arcadia was prominent, the Thebans under their great leaders invaded the Peloponnesus and threatened Sparta. But they did not reduce that ancient and illustrious city, which was defended by Agesilaus. Turning away, they wasted the region with sword and flame, receiving many helots and serfs into their ranks. The restoration of Messenia, and the fortification of its citadel Ithome, were the principal results of this three months' campaign in the south. Eluding the army of Iphicrates, sent by Athens to cut off his march northward, Epaminondas repassed the Isthmus, and went home—to find himself, in conjunction with Pelopidas and the other generals, on trial under a capital charge for having retained the command four months longer than the legal time. They were all acquitted; but there was much of malice and meanness in the charge.

369 B.C.

A second expedition of Epaminondas into the Peloponnesus, and a movement of Pelopidas northward to Thessaly, where the tyrants of Pheræ had grown formidable, were the principal events of the next year. Pelopidas was made prisoner by Alexander of Pheræ, but Epaminondas forced the Thessalian to release him.

His zeal in defending Thessaly from the oppression of Alexander cost Pelopidas his life. He had gathered an army for this expedition, but an eclipse of the sun spread such terror in the ranks, that he went northward with merely a handful of horse. At Pharsalus he got some soldiers, and met Alexander at Cynoscephalæ, where two steep hills in a plain were fiercely fought for by the contending armies. Pelopidas threw the foe into confusion; but, running rashly too far in advance in his eagerness to engage Alexander in single combat, he went within range of the hostile spears, and was transfixed, even through his armour, by the javelins of Alexander's guards. Great sorrow filled all Thessaly and Thebes at the loss of this hero.

364 B.C.

Meanwhile Arcadia, no longer the ally of Thebes, had been warring with Sparta and with Elis. In the latter struggle the Arcadians obtained possession of the temple at Olympia, where great treasures were amassed; and there was a difference of opinion as to whether these should or should not be applied to the payment of the troops. Mantinea headed the party, which condemned the sacrilege; and this

feeling grew so powerful in the Arcadian assembly that a peace was arranged with Elis. A Theban officer, stationed at Tegea, dreading the effect of such a measure, arrested certain men of rank who supported it. Mantinea took up the cause of Arcadian freedom, and cried out for his death, although he released the prisoners. Epaminondas
362 B.C. appeared upon the scene with a large army, and made an unsuccessful attempt on Sparta. At Mantinea he encountered a host, in which the Arcadians occupied the right wing, the Athenians the left, and the Spartans the right centre. In the arrangement of his men he took the prow of a galley as his model for both horse and foot. The event proved his wisdom, for the point of the cavalry charge left a gap in the enemy's line, into which the wedge-shaped phalanx plunged with destructive effect. But just then a spear point pierced his breast, and the breaking shaft left the head in the wound. Carried to a hillock, he continued to gaze with filmed eye upon the field, and, when he thought that victory had crowned the Theban arms, he allowed the fatal blade to be extracted: a great life rushed forth with the welling blood.

All the Grecian states, except Sparta, who would not acknowledge the independence of Messenia, made peace in the following year.

Sparta lost Agesilaus at this time, for, having gone upon an expedition to Egypt, he was driven during his return by a storm to the African shore, where he died at an extreme old age.

Thus, by the cutting down of the great men of Southern Greece, room was made for the soldiers of Macedonia, who now come upon the stage of Grecian history, and with the narrative of whose deeds the two following chapters shall be occupied.

GREAT NAMES OF GRECIAN LITERATURE, &c.

SECOND PERIOD.

SOPHOCLES, Attic tragedian—born at Colonus 495 B.C.—defeated Æschylus in 468—one of the Ten Strategi under Pericles in the Samian War—wrote one hundred and thirty plays—only seven extant, among which are *Antigone, Ajax, Œdipus Tyrannus, Œdipus at Colonus*—died in 406 B.C.

PHIDIAS, great sculptor—born at Athens about 490 B.C.—friend of Pericles, whose foes contrived his impeachment for peculation and impiety—died in prison 432 B.C.—chief works, Statue of the *Olympian Zeus,* and that of *Athene* in the *Parthenon.* Ictinus and Callicrates were the architects of the Parthenon.

HERODOTUS, Greek historian, called the Father of History—born at Halicarnassus in Caria, 484 B.C.—travelled much in Europe, Asia, and Africa—settled ultimately at Thurii in Italy, where he died—author of a *History of the Persian Wars* to the taking of Sestos, 478 B.C.

EURIPIDES, tragic poet—born at Salamis 480 B.C., on the very day of the battle—lived at Athens and the court of Archelaus, King of Macedon—friend of Socrates—torn to pieces by dogs in Macedon in 406 B.C.—eighteen plays extant, among them, *Medea, Orestes, Iphigeneia at Aulis, Iphigeneia at Tauri, Helena, Hecuba, Ion.*

THUCYDIDES, Greek historian—born 471 B.C.—owned gold mines in Thrace—commanded seven ships at Thasus in 424—lived twenty years in exile—author of a *History of the Peloponnesian War* until its twenty-first year.

SOCRATES, Athenian philosopher—born 469 B.C.—a member of the Five Hundred in 406—impeached for corruption of youth and heresy—the originator of formal logic—drank hemlock 399 B.C.

HIPPOCRATES, celebrated physician—born at Cos about 460 B.C.—travelled much in Greece—died at Larissa in Thessaly, about 357—The works assigned to Hippocrates were written by several persons.

ARISTOPHANES, comic poet—born probably at Athens about 444 B.C.—caricatured the leading men and events of his day, especially Cleon, and the Peloponnesian War—died about 380 B.C.—eleven comedies extant, among which are the *Knights,* the *Clouds,* the *Wasps,* the *Birds,* the *Frogs, Plutus* (first and second). Cratinus and Eupolis were the other great writers of the Old Comedy.

XENOPHON, Athenian historian—born about 444 B.C.—pupil of Socrates—commanded the Ten Thousand in their famous retreat—died probably at Corinth—chief works, the *Anabasis* and the *Cyropædia*—wrote also *Hellenica* and the *Memorabilia* of Socrates.

PLATO, Athenian philosopher—born 428 B.C.—pupil of Socrates—travelled in Egypt and Italy—taught under the trees of the Academy at Athens—became founder of the Academic School—died 347 B.C.—His works are in the form of *Dialogues*. There was another Plato, a comic poet of Aristophanes' time.

ZEUXIS, a painter of Heraclea—flourished 424–400 B.C.—came to Athens during the Peloponnesian War—chief work, his *Helen*.

PARRHASIUS, the painter of Ephesus, was somewhat younger. The contest between them is worth noting. Zeuxis painted grapes so well that birds came to pick them. Parrhasius brought out his picture with what seemed to be a curtain over it. Zeuxis called out to him to draw the curtain aside; but Parrhasius, triumphing in the success of his deception, pointed out that it was merely the painted image of a curtain.

THIRD PERIOD.

CHAPTER I.

PHILIP OF MACEDON.

Capture of Amphipolis. | The Social War. | Sacred War begins. | Philip Invades Thessaly. | The First Philippic. | Capture of Olynthus. | Doom of Phocis. | War with Athens. | Seizure of Elatea. | Battle of Chæronea. | Murder of Philip.

THE kingdom of Macedonia first emerges into historical prominence in the reign of Archelaus, about half a century before Philip made his own name and that of his country famous. It was a happy mixture of highland and lowland—green hills clothed with timber, and fertile valleys rich in grain, but richer in metallic wealth below the soil.

Philip, the third son of Amyntas, ascended the throne in 359 B.C., upon the death of his brother, who was slain in war with the Illyrians. Philip was either then or had lately been a hostage at Thebes, an abridgment of his liberty which he seems to have turned to good account in the culture of his mind, much as did the First James of Scotland during his detention at the English court. He studied Greek philosophy and literature, attracting the favourable regards of Plato, laying the foundation of his friendship with Aristotle, and observing the grain of the Greek character and the working of Grecian politics.

When he ascended the Macedonian throne, he set himself to make his army worthy of his ambition. Putting his soldiers beneath a system of iron discipline, he arranged them in that solid mass of men, which took the name of Phalanx from the resemblance of their ranks to lines of wooden rollers laid parallel. This body of infantry under him and his great son probably consisted of sixteen thousand men. He had also a Royal Guard, composed of the flower of the young nobility.

After defeating the Illyrians and crushing a pretender to the throne, whom the Athenians supported, he turned his eyes upon Amphipolis. This city at the mouth of the Strymon was prized by the Athenians chiefly for the neighbouring timber forests; and it had long been one of their most important possessions in the northern Ægean. They were now most anxious to recover it. Philip, who regarded it as a key to greater conquests, pretended to the Athenians that he did not mean to keep it when taken; and accordingly was permitted unhindered by them to carry it by storm (358 B.C.) He then proceeded to occupy Pydna: and, as a kind of bribe to keep Olynthus quiet, he made that place a present of Potidæa. The establishment of a military colony, henceforth called Philippi, in the centre of a rich mining district, added to his strength.

The Athenians were forced to look on these movements with little power to resist them. For their chief allies in the Ægean Confederacy had declared their intention of shaking off the Athenian yoke and paying tribute no longer, being galled to this revolt by Athenian insolence and corruption. Chios, Rhodes, and Byzantium led the opposition in this Social War, as it has been named. It continued for two years (357 B.C.–355 B.C.)

The Athenians laid siege to Chios, where Chabrias, one of their best admirals, pushed his ship with gallant hardihood into the port, and fell sword in hand, losing not only his life but the battle. A new fleet under Iphicrates and Timotheus, with whom Chares was associated in the command, went to Samos; and afterwards to the Hellespont. Meeting the enemy, the two former would not fight; upon which Chares lodged a complaint against them, and they were recalled, leaving him sole admiral. In urgent need of food and money, Chares, in return for a supply, gave assistance to Artabazus, a rebellious satrap, then in peril. This so enraged the Persian King that he began to prepare an armament in aid of the Allies. Athens then hurried to conclude a peace at any cost. She lost control of the principal islands in the Ægean; and lost too her hold on the important island of Corcyra.

The Phocian or Sacred War, which began in 357 B.C., soon afforded Philip an opportunity of interfering in the affairs of Greece. It originated in a jealous feeling that had long existed between Thebes and Phocis. Having obtained the ascendency in the Amphictyonic Council, which, though possessing a mere shadow of influence, still held its meetings, the Thebans contrived to have the Phocians condemned to pay a heavy fine, because they had sacrilegiously cultivated some portion of a plain, which had been doomed to lie waste for ever. Depending on Sparta, Phocis disregarded the sentence: and Philomelus the Phocian 357 B.C.
with two thousand men suddenly seized Delphi. The Locrians of Amphissa, coming to the rescue, were defeated by this daring leader, who proclaimed that his only object was to reinstate the Phocians in their rights, as guardians of the oracle, and that he had no intention of taking the treasures of the temple. All Northern Greece rose in arms against the sacrilegious chief: Athens and Sparta, though friendly to the Phocian cause, were too much occupied with their own affairs—the former with the Social War, the latter with Messene and Megalopolis—to give them more than good wishes. Philomelus, when he found the Thebans assembling a great allied army against him, laid hands on the Delphic treasure, and by its charms attracted to his banner a host of the worst profligates in Greece. The armies met near Neon in a valley of Parnassus, where the Phocians were defeated, and Philomelus died, either in the battle, or by leaping over a precipice.

His place was taken by his brother Onomarchus, who contrived to draw part of the army safely off to Delphi. This man by lavish gifts drew new recruits from various quarters; and with a strengthened force invaded Bœotia, but with slight success.

It was then that Philip resolved to interfere. 352 B.C.
Thessaly lay between him and the scene of conflict; but the capture of Methone on the Thermaic Gulf afforded him an entrance into that state. His march was directed against the tyrant of Pheræ. Onomarchus, appearing

as an ally, was at first successful in driving Philip back ; but the martial Macedonian King soon returned with a large army, all crowned with laurel-leaves in token of the sacred service in which they were engaged on behalf of the Delphic god. On the shore of the Pagasæan Gulf Onomarchus was completely defeated in sight of an Athenian squadron. The Phocian general, following the example of many of his soldiers, tried to swim to the Athenian ships, but perished in the attempt. Philip's victory left him master of Thessaly. Endeavouring to press southward by way of Thermopylæ, he found an Athenian force guarding the pass ; and, being refused permission to advance, thought it better to turn back in the meantime.

It was about this time that Demosthenes, the famous Athenian orator, and Philip's greatest foe, appeared upon the stage of history. Born about 385 B.C. he had the misfortune, when only seven years of age, to lose his father, a sword-cutler. While struggling through a weakly boyhood, he was kindled into a passionate love of oratory by hearing Callistratus speak ; and was put under the tuition of Isæus, being unable, it is stated, to pay the larger sum charged by Isocrates. His first speeches were directed against the fraudulent trustees, who had embezzled his patrimony : and after some delay he obliged these knaves to disgorge part of their spoil. But he had many and great obstacles to contend with. History presents no stronger lesson of the value of perseverance than that to be drawn from the story of this great rhetorician. At first his uncouth gestures and violent manner, his confused language and stammering tongue excited peals of laughter, when he ventured to address a public assembly; and many a time he crept homeward with covered head, smarting to the quick with the thought that a drunken sailor was listened to with more respect than he. The encouragement of one or two sagacious critics, who saw the volcanic fire glowing under an unpromising crust, induced him to devote himself to intense study. Building a chamber under ground, he shut himself into it, often for months at a time, with a head half shaven, so that he could not appear in public. By keeping pebbles in his mouth he corrected his stammering—by speaking amid the noise of waves he acquired that pitch of voice necessary to rise above the hum and roar of a public meeting—declaiming as he ran up hill strengthened his breathing—practice before a mirror improved his action. Thucydides, whose History he copied eight times, was the model, upon whom he formed his style. And so careful was he of his reputation that he never committed himself to an extempore speech, but prepared every word beforehand, provoking from his rivals the taunt, "that his arguments all smelled of the lamp."

Philip excited much anxiety at Athens by besieging Heræum on the Propontis, a step which seemed to indicate his intention of attacking the Chersonese. The Athenians were preparing an armament, when the news of Philip's illness came. During all the winter that ensued, Demosthenes was thinking deeply of the Macedonian scheme, and early in the next year he delivered the first of those twelve great orations, which from their purpose to excite the Athenians against Philip received the name of *Philippics*—a word afterwards used as a common term for any fierce invective. Demosthenes had many political enemies among the Athenian orators: the austere and impassive Phocion being the most formidable at this time. While the Athenians were employed in an expedition into Eubœa, where their sway was for a time restored, attention was attracted by Philip's movements with regard to Olynthus. First capturing the other Chalcidian towns, he gradually drew near the place he most of all coveted. Three embassies went from Olynthus to Athens; and three orations were delivered by Demosthenes, who in the last told his countrymen that they would have to choose between war at Olynthus and war at their own doors. It was during the siege of a Chalcidian town that an arrow struck Philip's eye, having an iambic verse attached to the shaft, expressing the aim of the archer. Treachery at last opened the gates of Olynthus to Philip; upon which, to secure his conquest of the trident peninsula, he razed it to the ground.

351 B.C.

348 B.C.

Philip then began to profess a desire for peace. An embassy, of which Demosthenes and Æschines his rival were prominent members, went from Athens to Pella: and after much discussion in both capitals the Athenians accepted Philip's terms, leaving in his hand their much-valued Amphipolis. In a common inn at Pheræ, whither the Athenian envoys followed him, he signed the peace, upon condition that Phocis was to be excluded from its benefits. Immediately afterwards he passed Thermopylæ, and with the aid of Theban and Thessalian allies ravaged Phocis (346 B.C.) The Athenians began to repair the fortifications of the Piræus in their dismay. Phocis suffered heavily. The people of twenty-two cities were scattered among the villages, and their old homes were levelled to the dust, while the state was condemned to pay a yearly tribute of sixty talents to the temple of Delphi, until the stolen treasure was made good. The seat of Phocis and her two votes in the Amphictyonic Council were given to Philip and his successors: a seemingly slight gain, but one which stamped the Macedonian King—hitherto looked upon as a semi-barbarian—with the privileges of a Greek citizen. It must have been a sore humiliation to fastidious and refined Athens to behold this warrior of the north exulting in his new-won position, as President of the Pythian games. But Athens was scarcely ready yet for the field. The Sacred War was now at an end.

One of Philip's favourite projects was to open a communication with the Peloponnesus, at that time much convulsed by the struggles of Sparta with Megalopolis and Messene. The condition of Elis affording him an opportunity of interfering, he tried to penetrate to the peninsula in two ways—first by an attack on Megara, and secondly by an invasion of Epirus; but the efforts of the Athenians and his wars in Thrace turned him from this enterprise in the meantime.

Demosthenes continued to stir the Athenians to action by his Philippics; and an expedition in 341 B.C. under Phocion paralyzed the Macedonian interest in Eubœa.

The actual collision between Philip and the Athenians occurred in the north. In the year 340 the Mace-
340 B.C. donian King laid siege to the important cities of Perinthus and Byzantium—the former a terraced

town upon a promontory of the Propontis, the latter well known as the old site of modern Stamboul. An Athenian armament under Phocion forced him to abandon the enterprise, to his great chagrin and the unbounded exultation of Athens. In gratitude colossal statues were erected in Byzantium; and some other towns presented a golden crown to the state, that had come forward as the champion of Greek freedom, 339 B.C.

Philip then undertook an expedition against the Scythians, who dwelt by the mouths of the Danube. He was prompted to this enterprise probably both by the hope of plunder, and the necessity of concealing his personal interest in a political intrigue then ripening into a new Sacred War, which he was cunningly kindling for his own purposes. On his return from his Scythian tour he found himself elected general-in-chief of an Amphictyonic army, deputed to make war upon the Amphissians, who had impiously tilled part of the plain of Cirrha.

Passing through Thermopylæ with an army larger than was needful, he lingered for a time in the heart of Greece—then suddenly seized Elatea, and began to fortify it. The value of this place depended on its position, which commanded the gorges entering Phocis and Bœotia from the north. The seizure of Elatea struck a sudden thrill of alarm through Greece; and the scales fell suddenly from eyes blinded hitherto to Philip's real aims. When the news reached Athens, the market-place was cleared with such haste that the wicker-stalls of the dealers were burned, and people were crowding to the Pnyx by day-break to hear what Demosthenes would say. His voice was for a treaty with Thebes, to the exclusion of all bitterness and rivalry; and his advice was followed. While these great allies were gathering their forces, Demosthenes went to several other states exhorting them to arm in the cause of Greece.

Philip in 338 B.C. proceeded to accomplish the nominal object of his expedition by taking the city of Amphissa, which he completely destroyed.

The decisive battle was fought on the plain of Chæronea, through which the brook Hæmus finds its way to the Cephisus. The omens at Athens were unfavourable; but Demosthenes, urgent for immediate battle, reminded the

Thebans of Epaminondas, the Athenians of Pericles, and with words of fire exhorted them to emulate the valour of these heroes. The orator went to battle himself, bearing a shield, on which in golden characters glittered the words, "To Good Fortune." The issue of the day was decided by Alexander, the son of Philip, then a youth of eighteen, who led a wing of the Macedonian army with such force as to break the array of the allies. In vain the Sacred Band laid down their lives where they stood. A torrent of flight set in; and among the fugitives was Demosthenes.

Aug., 338 B.C.

Athens at once began to prepare for a siege. Olive-trees were hewn down; stones were taken even from the tombs to repair the walls; and arms, hung in the temples, were seized for war. The conduct of Philip after the battle, when he went drunk into the field and sang some words of Demosthenes' decree in mockery over the Athenian dead, was in striking contrast with his moderate treatment of the Athenian prisoners, whom he sent home without ransom, and many of them with new clothes. Peace was offered to Athens, on terms which the people were glad to accept, although they were obliged to yield nearly all their foreign possessions. Thebes was treated much more severely. The government of the state was put into the hands of the exiles, who were recalled; and the citadel was occupied by a Macedonian garrison.

On the invitation of Philip a congress of the Grecian states was held at Corinth. Sparta alone was not represented by a minister. Here Philip declared his design of making war with Persia. The proposal was warmly received, and arrangements were made for raising a great armament. The victorious Macedonian then made a progress through the Peloponnesus for the purpose of humbling the Spartans, who had no resource but in submission.

The last years of Philip's life were darkened by domestic trouble. Having married Cleopatra, the niece of a general Attalus, Philip gave a great feast, at which Attalus expressed a hope that a son of his niece might be Philip's successor. Young Alexander, the son of Olympias, another of Philip's wives, was present; and with angry words flung the beaker, he was drinking from, at the head of Attalus. There was a great uproar. Philip, catching up his sword, plunged forward to stab Alexander, but he had drunk too much wine, and fell on the ground. "See," cried Alexander, pointing to the prostrate King, while a sneer curled his lip, "the man, who would pass from Europe to Asia, cannot go from one couch to another without falling." Placing his mother Olympias at the court of Epirus, Alexander then took refuge in Illyria.

A hollow reconciliation having been brought about, Alexander and his mother returned to the Macedonian court. A first instalment of the invading army crossed to Asia Minor, for the purpose of gaining over the Greek cities there; and in the spring of 336 B.C. all was ready for the great Persian expedition to set forth. The Delphic oracle had given a response, which might be twisted into encouragement. Philip resolved now to solemnize with great splendour the marriage, by the promise of which he had attracted Olympias back to Macedon. It was a union between Alexander of Epirus, and Cleopatra, the daughter of that hot-tempered lady. Part of the ceremonial, which took place at Ægæ, consisted of a theatrical spectacle; and Philip, unguarded that all might be able to admire his snowy robe and the majestic grace with which he bore the rose-crown on his head, was marching proudly in the centre of a gorgeous procession towards his throne, when a young man named Pausanias, rushing from among the crowd, drew a Celtic claymore from below his cloak and ran the monarch through the body. Philip fell dead, his white robe dyed in blood. The assassin fled towards the city gate, where horses stood bridled for flight. But a projecting vine-root caught the thong of his sandal, and he fell. Before he could mount, he was killed by the royal guards.

Thus perished Philip of Macedon in his forty-seventh year, cut off in the blossom of his fame, while the great scheme of his martial ambition was unfolding itself to a propitious commencement. The vindictive Olympias and her son Alexander, who now entered upon his great career, are not free from the suspicion of having had something to do with the murder.

336 B.C.

CHAPTER II.

ALEXANDER THE GREAT.

ALEXANDER the Great was born at Pella in 356 B.C. He grew up—a fair-haired rosy boy, until at the age of thirteen his father placed him under the tuition of Aristotle, the celebrated philosopher of Stagira, who instructed the prince for three years in politics, medicine, and other branches of knowledge. It was the hand of this great master that enriched with notes the copy of Homer's Iliad, which Alexander was wont to have beneath his pillow with his sword, and which he enshrined in a jewelled perfume-casket taken from Darius. The daring spirit of the boy was displayed in the taming of the horse Bucephalus, as related by Plutarch. A Thessalian dealer came to Philip, offering to sell the animal for about £2000. But none of the grooms could venture near, much less mount him; upon which the King refused to buy him. Alexander was displeased at this, and, amid the laughter of all the nobles, laid a wager of the price with his father that he would succeed in taming the steed. The prince had already noticed how Bucephalus was frightened at his own shadow; so turning the horse's head to the sun, he sprang, after some soothing words, on the animal's back, nor drew rein until a long gallop at full speed had subdued the fierce spirit of the steed. Philip welcomed his son back with tears of joy.

Such was the prince, who at the age of twenty ascended the throne of Macedon, 336 B.C. The first two years of his reign were spent in consolidating his position in Greece. After crushing some enemies at home, he advanced southward, for Athens was beginning hostile negotiations against him. Having received from the Amphictyonic Council at Thermopylæ the chief command of their armies, he paused before Thebes. His presence was enough. Athens sent a submissive embassy and all became quiet.

Alexander then undertook a northern campaign. Subduing first the Thracians, who vainly rolled their waggons down upon his march, he crossed Mount Hæmus, defeated the Triballi, and even carried his banner victoriously over the Danube among the wild Getes. Barbarians of all kinds crowded round to seek his good-will, among them big Celts from the Adriatic, who, when he asked "What they feared most?" proudly answered, "Lest the sky should fall." His march was then directed into Illyria, where a strong fortress, Pellion, encircled with forests, invited his attack. While beginning to invest this place, a hostile army forced him to retreat; but, coming suddenly back, he surprised and routed the Illyrians, and forced their king to burn the fortress and flee.

While Alexander was in this wild region, a report of his death spread through Greece, to the joy and relief of many states. The Thebans besieged the Macedonian garrison in the Cadmea; and Athens was ready to aid in the enterprise, when the Macedonian came like a thunderbolt amongst them, having marched over rock and river for a fortnight. The Thebans still ventured to resist, upon which he invested the city. Repelling a sally, his troops entered one of the gates with the flying foe. A dreadful massacre followed. The city was all levelled to the music of flutes, except the Cadmea, in which a Macedonian garrison was placed, and the house of Pindar, which the victor spared in memory of the poet. The blood of the slaughtered Thebans afterwards hung heavy upon Alexander's soul: and to the anger of avenging Bacchus he superstitiously ascribed many of his crimes and misfortunes.

335 B.C.

Athens expected to undergo similar treatment; but Alexander contented himself with demanding nine of his leading opponents, Demosthenes among the number. Even this demand he did not press, for a mightier project filled his mind—to realize the rudely interrupted dream of his father Philip by achieving the conquest of Asia.

With a force of little more than thirty thousand foot and five thousand horse he proceeded to the Hellespont early in 334 B.C., having only seventy talents in his money-chests, but boundlessly rich in *Hope*, as he told Perdiccas, who wondered at his lavish distribution of the farms and houses and other items of the crown property. Antipater was left with an army to manage Macedonia and Greece. The army under Parmenio crossed from Sestos to Abydos; but Alexander sailed from Elæus, and, as his galley neared the shore, hurled a javelin into the Asian sand, and sprang from the bulwarks in complete armour.

His first visit was to the plain of Troy. At Sigeum he poured oil and laid a chaplet reverently on the pillar of Achilles, his favourite hero. But sterner work awaited him. Advancing to the Granicus, a small stream running from Mount Ida to the Propontis, he found two satraps posted there with twenty thousand Greek mercenaries and an equal number of native horse. Parmenio advised him against attempting the passage so late in the day; but Alexander replied, "The Hellespont would blush, if, after having passed it, we should fear the Granicus." Sending the cavalry into the stream, he followed with the Phalanx, moving aslant across the current under showers of Persian arrows. With difficulty they struggled up the steep and muddy banks. His gilded shield and the double white plume waving from his crest made Alexander a conspicuous mark, and in the mellay a javelin pierced the joint

334 B.C.

of his cuirass, but without wounding him. A closer risk than this befell him. Charging a Persian noble in the breast, he brought him to the ground; but almost at the same moment an axe descended on his own head, shearing half his plume away and cutting through the helmet down to his very hair. The giver of this blow Alexander struck from his horse with a spear-wound in the breast. But behind him a third Persian officer had swung a scimitar on high to finish what the axe had left undone, when the faithful Cleitus with a rapid sabre-stroke lopped the uplifted arm from the shoulder, and saved the King. When the Persians were driven back, the Greek mercenaries held their ground, but they were soon surrounded and slaughtered. Alexander sent home some magnificent spoils as the first-fruits of his enterprise. Three hundred suits of armour went to Athens, with an inscription, which ascribed the honour of their capture to Alexander and all the Greeks, *except the Lacedæmonians.*

Space will not permit us to follow minutely the march of Alexander through Asia Minor. After receiving the submission of Sardis and Ephesus, he reduced Miletus and Halicarnassus. The man he regarded as most formidable in those regions was Memnon of Rhodes, whom however illness cut off in the following year, while besieging Mitylene. From Caria he sent home part of his army to spend the winter and tell of the glorious success he had achieved. He then pursued a curving course round the shores of Caria and Lycia. At the jutting point called Climax, on the latter coast, he courted a perilous adventure by marching with a chosen few round the base of the cliffs, while a south wind drove a heavy surf over the path. Luckily the wind went round to the north, an occurrence from which he drew the luckiest omens, and even then his men had to wade breast-high for a whole day. His main army was meanwhile toiling over the ridge by a rugged winding way. He then struck due north through Pisidia and Phrygia to Gordium, why it is not very clear, unless that it was a convenient place to effect a junction with the troops returning from Macedonia, and his new levies, amounting to three thousand foot and six hundred and fifty horse. The citadel of Gordium contained the celebrated waggon of Midas, the yoke of which was fastened to the pole by a remarkable knot, made of the bark of the cornel-tree. There was a legend to the effect that he who untied the knot should conquer Asia. This prophecy Alexander fulfilled, either by an impatient chop of his sword, as writers of dramatic taste love to announce, or by the more common-place plan of drawing out a peg, which fastened the yoke to the beam. Hence the proverb about "cutting the Gordian knot." His march soon turned southward through Galatia and Cappadocia to the city of Tarsus in Cilicia, where he stayed a while.

This delay was partly owing to a fever, caught, it is said, by bathing while heated in the clear cold stream of Cydnus, on which Tarsus stands. While under the treatment of Philip the physician he received a letter from Parmenio, stating that a report was abroad through the camp that Darius had bribed Philip to poison him. The King crushed the letter below his pillow, and, when Philip came in with a cup of medicine, looked him steadily in the eyes, handed him the scroll, and drank off the potion. The result proved Philip's fidelity. Speech and motion deserted the patient for a time—life and health then began to flow back—and in some days the King was well enough to show his wan and wasted face to the anxious soldiery.

At Mallus on the Gulf of Issus, close to the north-eastern angle of the Levant, Alexander first heard of the approach of Darius the Persian king. For many years the Persian court had been a scene of crime and bloodshed. The power had lately sunk into the hands of a eunuch named Bagoas, an infamous king-maker and king-slayer, who placed Darius Codomannus on the throne in the year 336 B.C., the very year of Alexander's accession. Darius, finding that Bagoas was quietly preparing for him a poison-draught similar to that which had left the throne lately vacant, turned the eunuch's villany on himself and made him drink the death he had mixed for so many.

The army of Darius, consisting of six hundred thousand warriors, dragged after it in a cumbrous but gorgeous train the thousand appendages of ancient Oriental luxury,—silver altars on which scarlet-robed *Magi* tended the sacred flame—waggons full of women and children—treasure-chests—cooks—confectioners—perfumers—garland-weavers—dancers—singers—and countless other ministers to magnificent indolence.

Alexander, marching through a maritime pass previously cleared by Parmenio, had reached Issus and had gone through the gates dividing Syria from Cilicia, when he heard that Darius was following in his rear. The Persian king, marching behind the mountains in a direction parallel but opposite to the line of Alexander's progress, had come down to the coast by a pass called the Amanic Gates. Believing Alexander to be in flight, he pursued, and encamped, where the torrent called Pinarus trenches and breaks the narrow plain of Issus between the mountains and the sea. It was a glorious movement for Alexander, for on that contracted field the huge size of the Persian host would prove anything but an advantage.

In a skilful speech the Macedonian king reminded his men of the Ten Thousand, and the ancient triumphs of Grecian freemen over Persian slaves. After some
manœuvring he led his men forward, himself in 333
command of the right wing. The Phalanx advanced B.C.
slowly, until the buzzing flights of Persian arrows stung it into speed. There was some disorder caused by the passage of the river, and the lagging of the divisions on the left; and in the movements of the Phalanx compact order was essential.* As at the Granicus the Greek mercenaries made the boldest stand on the Persian side; but Alexander, victorious over the left wing, took them in flank, upon which Darius whipped his horses from the field. His loyal subjects followed; and the crush and slaughter in the northern pass were terrible. Alexander was slightly wounded in the thigh, but he followed Darius to the foot of the hills, where the Persian leaped from his chariot and took horse. Returning with the chariot, the victor bathed in the royal bath, and supped in the royal tent of Darius. In the midst of his festivity the noise of weeping caught his ear: it was the mourning of Sisygambis and Statira, the mother and the wife of the Persian monarch. To his honour be it said, he sent them a message of comfort; and treated them with a delicate kindness the Orientals were not used to experience at the hands of conquerors. The capture of Damascus, whither Darius had sent the bulk of his treasures, was an immediate result of the victory of Issus.

Marching through Phœnicia, all quite submissive, Alexander came to Tyre, which, proud of her maritime fame and strongly seated on the sea, defied his attack. This famous city was built upon an island, severed from the shore by a

* The Phalanx was generally composed of sixteen or eighteen thousand men, arrayed sixteen deep. They carried, besides a long sword, the *sarissa*, a spear of twenty-four feet; and the ranks were so placed, that each man in the front line was guarded on each side by *six* spear-heads, projecting at different distances, and forming an almost impenetrable hedge. The ten hinder ranks carried their spears upright, until a gap was made in front.

stormy channel half a mile wide. Walls of solid masonry one hundred and fifty feet high, rose from the cliffs which faced the land. The city was well supplied with food; several springs gushed up within the walls; and the inhabitants were both courageous and clever in all that related to nautical matters. The two harbours, north and south, were defended by a fleet of galleys.

Alexander commenced to build a mole or pier across the channel in order to reach the walls; and for a time all went well. But, as the mole advanced, the workmen came within shot of the walls and the galleys; and were sorely hindered in their toil. Towers, covered with hides and bearing engines on the top, were built to protect them; but the besieged, sending a fire-ship on whose blazing masts hung pots of burning liquid, destroyed these structures, while the crews of their boats tore up the foundations of the mole. Alexander then got a fleet of two hundred and fifty sail at Sidon, and invested the city on the seaward side, causing the Tyrian galleys to shrink into the harbours. The

332 B.C.

progress of the attacking fleet was hindered by a mass of stones thrown into the channel; and, while the besiegers were lifting these sunken rocks, Tyrian divers constantly cut the ropes by which the ships were anchored. The adoption of chain cables removed this difficulty. Another mode of annoying the besiegers invented by the Tyrians, was the flinging of shieldfuls of heated sand, which got between the joints of the armour of the Greeks and burned them to the bone.

At last the walls on the south side were breached, and, a calm day being chosen, a general assault took place. Alexander led the forlorn hope; and after a desperate struggle the place was carried by storm. At the same time both harbours were forced by the fleet. The seven months' siege was over; and the Tyrians underwent the usual doom of death and slavery.

Darius now thought fit to offer peace on certain terms, of which Parmenio said in the council, "Were I Alexander, I should accept them." The reply is famous and characteristic, "So should I, were I Parmenio."

Gaza, a city on a hill, with high walls, also resisted. It

was taken after three or four months' siege by making a huge mound, from which the engines battered the works. At this place Alexander was wounded in the shoulder by a dart from a machine.

Josephus relates a Jewish legend, probably true, to the effect that Alexander visited Jerusalem, near which he was met by the High-priest and all the Levitical order in their full vestments, accompanied by the mass of the people in white robes. Alexander, startled with the likeness of the High-priest to a reverend figure seen in a dream at Dium, approached and did homage with awe-struck face. Then, having sacrificed in the Temple after the Jewish fashion, he gave splendid gifts to priests and people, and departed on his southward way.

In Egypt he found the people most anxious to cast off the Persian yoke. There, upon a tongue of land between the sea and a spacious lake, and sheltered on the north by a rocky islet-ridge called Pharos, he found the little village of Racotis, on the site of which he marked out the foundation of the city still called by his name. There being no chalk to trace the walls, flour was scattered in a white
ring, upon which clouds of marsh-birds settled. 331
This the King interpreted into a favourable omen. B.C.
A light-house, twinkling on the point of Pharos,
soon guided ships to the havens on each side of the causeway connecting the island with the shore; and a canal brought the sweet Nile water into the subterranean cisterns of the place.

Alexander paid a visit to the Oasis of Ammon, where the priests hailed him as a son of Jove. It was a perilous journey over sands, which often rose and fell like sea-waves, whelming travellers in a scorching grave: but serpents and crows marshalled the victor on his way, and rain fell to beat the sand into a cool and hardened path.

After providing for the government of Egypt, Alexander returned to Phœnicia, and resumed his march towards the centre of the Persian empire. Crossing the Euphrates at Thapsacus, he advanced through the cooler and more fertile regions of Mesopotamia to the Tigris, over which he passed unhindered and then struck down stream. Darius awaited his approach not far off with an army, which some writers describe as amounting to a million of foot, and forty thousand horse. He had chosen his ground carefully at Gaugamela,* in a plain watered by the Bumodus, a feeder of the Lycus. His pioneers had been already smoothing the ground for the easier operation of his cavalry and his chariots.

Having allowed his men four days to rest, Alexander came in sight of the Persian host, filling the plain below, one morning shortly after dawn. It must have been an imposing spectacle. Round the splendid chariot of the King, who occupied the centre of the line, flashed the sabres of the royal kinsmen, and the golden globes of the foot-guards' lances. The elephants and the scythed chariots were drawn up in front. The Greek mercenaries stood arrayed on each side; while behind, like waves of various colours fading into distance, masses of men and horses, drawn from a hundred nations, rolled into the back-ground.

Parmenio advised Alexander to delay the battle, until he had surveyed the ground; to which the King assented. That night the same general proposed a surprise; but to this Alexander would not yield. When morning dawned, his officers had to waken the man, who that day was about to contend for the crown of Asia.

The Macedonian army amounted to only forty thousand foot and six thousand horse. The Phalanx was drawn up as usual in six divisions; but Alexander formed a second line, chiefly of light troops, for the purpose of baffling the flank movements of the Persian cavalry and the operations of their chariots. Upon this his hopes of victory largely depended.

Day broke upon the army of Darius tired and unrefreshed, for his soldiers had remained under arms all night, expecting an attack. The great danger, with which Alexander had to contend, was the being outflanked and enclosed by the huge stretching wings of the Persian host, which ex-
331 tended far beyond his comparatively short line.
B.C. To avert this he made a slanting movement of the right wing, which he led in person. In vain the

* The battle of Gaugamela is otherwise styled the battle of Arbela, although the latter, a considerable town, was twenty miles from the scene of conflict.

bands of Scythian and Bactrian horse strove to turn his flank: they were repelled and broken by his second line. The light troops, by slaying the drivers and horses, made the chariots worse than useless; or, by opening to let them pass, placed them in a position where they were easily taken. A side movement of the Persian horse left a gap, through which Alexander poured a pointed column. And then came the struggle of the Phalanx with the Persian centre.

Alexander, whose helmet and gorget of shining iron, cuirass of quilted linen, and belt embroidered with the costliest work of Helicon, made him a conspicuous figure, was accompanied by a soothsayer in a white robe and a crown of gold, who pointed to an eagle overhead as the charge began. Right at the royal chariot went the rush. The guards fled. A few, who waited the onset, were overturned, and clung in vain to the hoofs of the Grecian horses. Darius, seeing the wheels of his chariot clogged with corpses and the horses lashing wildly out, sprang off, and fled from the field on the back of a mare.

The left wing under Parmenio was in difficulties for a time; but the flight of Darius, and the bad generalship of the Persians, gave the Thessalian horse a fair opportunity of extricating him.

Darius escaped again, as he had escaped at Issus. His baggage and his treasures were found at Arbela by the victors. Thus ended the battle of Gaugamela, leaving Alexander master of Western Asia.

The luxurious revels of Babylon, and the splendid spoils of Susa, where the conqueror found some of the booty, carried away from Greece by Xerxes, delayed the advance of the army for a time, during which Alexander rewarded his veteran captains with military honours. Then, forcing his way through the Persian Gates, he came to Persepolis. There occurred the remarkable banquet-scene, which Dryden celebrated in his magnificent ode called *Alexander's Feast.* A woman, who took part in the revel, proposed to burn the palace of Xerxes; and Alexander, drunk with wine and carried away by the wild excitement of the orgies, snatched up a torch, and was the first to fire the doomed building, which soon sank in ashes.

The pursuit of Darius was then continued through Ecbatana* and Rhagæ. Bessus, the treacherous satrap of Bactria, had seized the Persian monarch; and, when Alexander at last came galloping up with a small band of men in armour, his foe lay dead in the chariot, where he had been previously chained, pierced with the darts of conspirators, whose flight he would not share. Alexander flung his cloak over the wreck of fallen glory, and turned away, let us hope, with a softened heart.

The satrap Artabazus submitted. The invasion of Hyrcania then occupied the victor's attention. He was fond of varying the toils of the way by hunting; and no ignoble game would serve his spear, which sought the lion rather than inferior beasts. In this region Bucephalus, which was reserved to bear his master only in the battle-field, was captured by the natives; but a threat of extermination induced them to return the steed. At Zadracarta Alexander beheld the Caspian, which he rashly concluded to be a branch of *Palus Mæotis* (the Sea of Azov).

About this time Alexander, for the purpose of securing more control over the Asiatics, and perhaps also of gratifying his own vanity, assumed the tiara, the dress, and the manners of a Persian king, to the great discontent of many of his generals and soldiers.

He then advanced through Parthia, bent upon crushing the traitor Bessus, who had also assumed the Persian tiara. During his progress he founded a city, Alexandria Ariorum, the *Herat* which has figured so often in the history of modern Asia, and whose position still makes it the centre of commerce in those regions.

At Prophthasia occurred one of the revengeful acts, which are the chief blots on the fame of Alexander. Philotas, the son of Parmenio and captain of the Horse-guards, being a boastful man, was in the habit sometimes in his cups of speaking slightingly of the "boy" Alexander. His mistress repeated some of this tipsy gossip; and Craterus, another favourite, made her tell the King. Philotas railed too at the pretensions of Alexander to celestial descent, and even went the length of writing him

* Said to be the modern Ispahan.

a letter of ironical congratulation on the subject. Becoming acquainted with a plot against the life of the King, he said nothing about it; and, when Alexander taxed him with this suspicious silence, he replied that he had looked upon the whole thing as too ridiculous for disclosure. The King shook hands with him in token of forgiveness; but a short time afterwards he was arrested and accused by Alexander in person. Being put to the torture, he made an improbable confession, involving his father Parmenio. And both were put to death.

Pursuing his journey, the King founded another Alexandria, now surviving in Candahar. His course was then directed across Paropamisus, or Hindoo-Koosh, into the basin of the Oxus. The snow was deep, and the supplies of food fell short, so that the soldiers were compelled to eat their beasts of burden, and a wild plant of the valleys called *silphium*. After the passage of the river Oxus Bessus was betrayed into the hands of Alexander, who sent him to Ecbatana. There are two accounts of his death. Bending young trees, his executioners tied him by the limbs to these, and then let them spring asunder, tearing him to pieces; or, placing him on a cross, they stabbed him to death with darts.

The most northerly limit of Alexander's march was the Jaxartes, a river falling into the Sea of Aral. In Sogdiana, between the two great feeders of that lake, he found a warlike race that gave him much trouble. Taking the Seven Fortresses, he fought his way on to the Jaxartes, which was lined with Scythians, whom with difficulty he drove back. In another quarter they defeated one of his officers; a reverse he felt sorely, for it was his first.

A memorable achievement in this region was the taking of the Sogdian Rock, a hill-fortress faced on all
sides by sharp cliffs, accessible by a mere thread of 328
a pathway, and provisioned for two years. The B.C.
mountain chief, when summoned to surrender, asked the Macedonians in a sneering tone, if they wore wings. Alexander offered a number of gold pieces to the first ten that reached the top. It was like scaling an Alpine peak.

Getting ropes and iron tent-pins, some of the best climbers made the attempt by night on the steepest side, driving the pins into the hard-frozen snow. The chieftain stared and trembled, when at dawn he saw the Greek flags waving on the summit; and he at once surrendered.

Among the captives was Roxana, daughter of Oxyartes, the Bactrian satrap. She became the wife, her father the close ally, of Alexander.

Alexander stained his royal name deeply at Maracanda, where his court remained for a time in 328 B.C. We have already heard of Cleitus. Appointed satrap of Bactria, he joined Alexander in a drinking-bout before he left the court; and, as the evening wore away and the wine mounted to the brains of the revellers, there arose a hot discussion, in which Cleitus ascribed to *all* the soldiers the glory Alexander deemed his own special due, and expressed an opinion that Philip was a greater soldier than his son. The King grew hot with rage; and when Cleitus, stretching out his hand, reminded Alexander whose life it had saved at the Granicus, the incensed monarch sprang from the couch. His friends held him back, while the foolish Cleitus was dragged from the room, still jibing as he went. Alexander broke from those who held him, snatched up a spear, and, meeting Cleitus at the door, struck its point into his body and killed him. Reäction was instant. For three days the King lay without food, gnawed by sharp remorse.

A short time afterwards, some of Alexander's pages having formed a plot to kill him, Callisthenes, a kinsman of Aristotle, suffered death for his connection with the conspiracy.

The march to India now began. The scene of Alexander's victory there was that fertile triangle, now called Punjaub, lying between the Indus and the Hyphasis or *Sutlej*. One of the native princes, called Taxiles from the name of his capital Taxila, invited him across the Indus to subdue another prince named Porus. Adding seventy thousand Asiatics to his ranks, which swelled his army to nearly one hundred and fifty thousand, he crossed the mountains to Cabul, and devoted a campaign to the subjugation of the mountain-tribes, taking among other places the rock-built Aornus.

327 B.C.

Having crossed the Indus at Attock, he remained for some time at Taxila, which he made the centre of a Macedonian province. On the further bank of the Hydaspes (now *Jhelum*) Porus took his post with a vast number of elephants. Alexander, seeing that stratagem was necessary, selected a wood about a mile higher, opposite an island tufted with trees, as a fitting place quietly to put the boats together and stuff the skins with straw, in preparation for crossing, while his horsemen with shouts and galloping up and down distracted the attention of Porus. Thus, by dividing his forces, Alexander got a portion of his army across the stream, after which was fought the great battle.

Porus, taking his station on a sandy tract, ranged his elephants before him. Alexander, with the right wing of his army, attacked the Indian left, which drew a mass of cavalry from the opposite extremity of the Indian line. These were taken in the rear at once by Cœnus and his horse. For a time the elephants made some impression on the Phalanx; but a second charge of the Macedonian horse rendered these animals unmanageable. The Phalanx parted to let the terror-stricken animals through; and Alexander completed the rout of the Indians by an advance of the whole line. Meanwhile Craterus was crossing; and his fresh troops carried on the pursuit vigorously. Porus, who rode on a highly-trained elephant, refused at first to submit, though wounded; but at length he yielded, asking only to be treated like a king. Alexander replaced him on his throne, and greatly enlarged his dominions.

326 B.C.

Two cities were founded in that region by the victor—*Nicaea* in honour of his triumph, and *Bucephala* in honour of his famous horse, which died there.

Crossing the other rivers of the Punjaub, the army reached the Hyphasis or *Sutlej*, the eastern limit of their march. There the desire of the army to return became so strong that Alexander was forced to yield. Much against his will, he found the sacrifices unfavourable to the passage of the stream; and, having built twelve great altars on the bank, he retraced his steps to the Hydaspes.

His wrights had already for some time been at work upon

cedar and fir, floated down from the mountains to build a fleet for the navigation of the Indus; and a flotilla of two thousand vessels soon began to glide down the broad bosom of the current, while the army marched along the banks. At the junction of the Chenab and the Jhelum the rapids and eddies caused alarm and loss, whirling the boats round, breaking their oars, and wrecking two galleys.

In a war against the Malli Alexander nearly lost his life. The breaking of a scaling-ladder left him with a few of his guards on the wall, and a rash leap into the town placed him alone against a host. After slaying several he received an arrow in the breast, and fell. Luckily, by sticking pegs into the hard mud of the rampart the Macedonians had meanwhile contrived to clamber over. They carried the King to his tent, and sawed off the wooden shaft; but there was great difficulty in extracting the barbed head from its lodgment in the bone. Some say Alexander made Perdiccas widen the gaping wound with his sword to permit the extraction of the iron. Fainting from loss of blood, he lay at the point of death for a time; but the strength of his constitution at last prevailed.

This passage down the river occupied seven months. On approaching the sea the galleys of exploration encountered fierce gales; and their crews, who in the Mediterranean had never seen any perceptible tide, were astonished at the violent ebb and flow of the ocean, which at one time left their galleys in the mud, and at another swept them high upon the shore.

Having explored the delta of the Indus in the ardour of his new ambition of geographical discovery, Alexander committed the care of the fleet to Nearchus, while with the mass of his army he proceeded westward through the desert of Gedrosia, thinly peopled on the sea-margin with a wretched race of fish-eaters. The sufferings of the army on this two months' march were dreadful. Scorching thirst—venomous serpents—shrubs with breath of poison and thorns like daggers—blistering rock below and a copper sky above—and winds that furrowed the whole expanse for miles into sweeping sand-billows, thinned their ranks and withered them into wretchedness, until the fair grape-land of Carmania by the Strait of Ormuz smiled a welcome to the worn survivors.

When settled down at Susa in 324 B.C., Alexander assumed more than ever the Persian style. In order to cement the union of the nations, he promoted the marriages of his officers with Persian women, setting an example by taking Statira the daughter of Darius to be his wife. The nuptial-banquets lasted for some days. At Opis on the Tigris the discontent of the army broke into open mutiny, which called for all his coolness and promptitude. The execution of the ringleaders, however, quelled the disturbance. He soon afterwards found it expedient to send home ten thousand veterans under the command of Craterus.

During a festival at Ecbatana a favourite named Hephæstion took sick of fever, and, by imprudently dining off roast fowl and wine, brought on his death. This was a heavy blow to the King, who went almost to the borders of the absurd in the splendour of his arrangements for the funeral at Babylon.

The young conqueror, now only thirty-three, was at this time in the very zenith of his fame. Envoys from the most distant countries were flocking to do homage at his court, and magnificent projects of new conquests, to begin with Arabia, were floating through his brain, when—he died. After a series of heavy drinking-bouts he took a bath, and caught a fever. At first he regarded it as trifling;
but in some days he became speechless; and his 323
soldiers passed in mournful single file through the B.C.
chamber, which was soon to be the abode of Death.
A feeble look and a tremulous shifting of the hands were all that remained of the imperial gesture, and the invincible thunder of command. His last action was to pull a ring from his finger, and give it to Perdiccas. So died one of the men, whom history dignifies with the title of Great.

CHAPTER III.

THE GENERALS OF ALEXANDER.

Demosthenes. — Lamian War. — Partition of Triparadisus. — Death of Phocion. — Four Years' War. — Demetrius at Athens. — Battle of Ipsus. — Demetrius in Macedonia.

BETWEEN the battle of Gaugamela and the death of Alexander the principal political event in Greece was a movement of Agis, King of Sparta, who advanced with a great army against Megalopolis. Antipater, the regent of Macedonia, hurrying southward, defeated him with great loss. When Agis saw that all was over, he continued fighting on one knee till he fell (330 B.C.).

In the same year the case of Æschines against Ctesiphon was decided against the former. Ctesiphon proposed that a crown of gold should be presented to Demosthenes for his public services, and that proclamation of the honour should be made in the theatre at the Dionysiac festival, when strangers filled the city. Æschines, a rival of Demosthenes, accused Ctesiphon of breaking the law by this proposal. The cause afforded opportunities for splendid displays of eloquence, and a plentiful use of invective. It was decided against Æschines, who retired in disgust to Rhodes.

But, six years later, Demosthenes became involved in an ugly transaction, which drove him into exile. Harpalus, the treasurer of Alexander at Ecbatana, having squandered his master's wealth, fled to Athens with a portion of the spoil, with which he bought over several of the orators. Demosthenes argued at first against his reception; but, it is stated, his scruples were overcome by a present consisting of a beautifully wrought goblet of gold, filled with golden coins. Next day he came to the assembly with woollen wrappers round his throat, apparently so hoarse
324 B.C. that he could not utter a word. There were some in the crowd, who cried out that he had swal-

lowed gold and silver, and others prayed for silence "to hear the man with the cup." At the urgent instance of Demosthenes the court of Areopagus investigated this case of alleged bribery; and Demosthenes himself was the first person convicted by them. In default of payment of fifty talents, he was put in prison; but, having escaped, he settled in Ægina, whence he often looked mournfully across at Athens. It is right to add that his guilt is still a disputed point.

About a year before his death Alexander had sent to Greece a letter, which was read to the crowds at Olympia, proclaiming that all exiles should be restored to their cities. This excited much opposition, especially at Athens. Leosthenes, having equipped an army, passed into Ætolia, and soon afterwards, meeting Antipater in the field, won a battle, chiefly owing to the desertion of the Thessalian horse from the Macedonian ranks. Antipater threw himself into Lamia, where he was blockaded by Leosthenes, who soon, however, died of a wound in his head inflicted by a stone. The arrival of Craterus with reinforcements turned the scale of war. Antipater with the aid of the veterans defeated the Athenians and Thessalians so signally in the battle of Crannon that the confederacy fell to pieces, and Athens was obliged to receive a Macedonian garrison into the Munychia, and to adopt a new constitution under the direction of Phocion. By the new system twelve thousand citizens were disfranchised; and most of them were drafted off to Thrace (322 B.C.).

323 B.C.

Demosthenes had been recalled before this, owing to the efforts which he continued to make against the Macedonians; but now he fled for refuge to the temple of Neptune in the island of Calaurea. Demades the orator proposed that all such fugitives should be doomed to death; and accordingly Archias, captain of the "Exile hunters," rowed over to this island to entice Demosthenes from the sanctuary. Retiring to the inner temple, the orator sat down as if to write a letter home, and, while biting the top of the reed-pen, as men will do when thinking ere they write, he was all the while sucking poison from its hollow centre. Another story states that he took something like gold from a scrap of linen, and put it into his mouth. The poison acted quickly. Trying to stagger to the door, he fell groaning by the altar, and so he died.

The Lamian War, as the two years' struggle is called, was now at an end.

The Alexandrian Empire fell to pieces amid bloodshed and war. For more than twenty years the generals of the fallen King contended fiercely for the fragments of his mantle. Perdiccas, to whom Alexander gave his ring, maintained a kind of regency for about a year; but his death in Egypt in 322 afforded an opportunity for the first Partition, called that of Triparadisus, from a town in Upper Syria.

322 B.C.

Ptolemy Lagus received Egypt—Seleucus got Babylonia—Asia Minor was left to Antigonus, who was charged with the war against Eumenes, appointed to that province by Perdiccas—Lysimachus established himself in Thrace—while Antipater managed the affairs of Macedonia and Greece.

Antipater, dying in 319, left the power to his friend Polysperchon rather than to his son Cassander. The latter, beginning to intrigue, soon caused Nicanor to seize the Piræus for him. Alexander, the son of Polysperchon, came to Athens also, as the people began to suspect, with sinister designs upon the city. The popular voice blaming Phocion loudly for all, he fled with some friends to the camp of Alexander, who gave him letters to Polysperchon. The old Macedonian sent him back to Athens bound with ropes: and amid the roaring of a crowded theatre this leader of Athenian aristocracy was sentenced to drink the fatal hemlock.

318 B.C.

Polysperchon then attempted without success to take Megalopolis; while his clever rival, holding the Piræus, induced the Athenians to listen to his terms. The city of Pericles then received, as its ruler, a guardian appointed by the Macedonian Cassander.

The victories of Antigonus over Eumenes, ending with the death of the latter, induced the triumphant general to assume the regency. This of course drew upon him the hostility of all the other generals; and a four years' war (315–311) ensued, during which in 312 Ptolemy defeated Demetrius Poliorcetes, son of Antigonus, at Gaza, and thus enabled Seleucus to recover Babylon.

Demetrius of Phalerum, being appointed by Cassander Guardian of Athens, ruled that city for eleven years (318–307), at first wisely, but afterwards with oppression and extravagance. It was therefore with sincere welcome that the Athenians greeted the approach of Demetrius Poliorcetes, the son of Antigonus, and the undoubted hero of this troubled time. The Phalerian 307 B.C. surrendered the city to this martial youth, who, after taking Munychia by storm, found himself master of the ancient centre of Grecian glory. From Athens Demetrius was recalled to the Levant, where by the capture of the city Salamis he wrested the island of Cyprus from Ptolemy. Antigonus after this victory assumed the title of King, and conferred it also on his beloved son; an example which his rivals, Ptolemy, Lysimachus, and Seleucus, were not slow to follow. Demetrius was not so successful in his expedition against Rhodes, upon which he exhausted all his skill and strength in vain.

Meanwhile the reconciliation of Cassander and Polysperchon had restored Macedonian rule in Greece. The latter overran the Peloponnesus successfully, while the former secured Corinth and laid siege to Athens. To the relief of Athens Demetrius Poliorcetes came with 303 B.C. three hundred and thirty sail. Defeating Cassander near Thermopylæ, he was greeted with the most fulsome flattery on his entrance into Attica. But the bloom was off his name. He lived within the city in a most profligate and shameless style, and began to display all the symptoms of incipient tyranny.

A league being formed by Cassander, Ptolemy, Seleucus, and Lysimachus against Antigonus and his son, a war began, which closed with the famous battle of Ipsus, fought near a little town in Phrygia. The battle was lost by the rashness of Demetrius, who pursued some routed 301 B.C. cavalry too far, and on his return found himself cut off from the main body by an impenetrable line of elephants. Antigonus, aged eighty, died on the field; Demetrius, soon afterwards, sailing from Ephesus in the hope of a welcome at Athens, was met by a message refusing to admit him.

The capture of the Thracian Chersonese and other successes enabled him, a few years later, to save Athens from Leochares, a tyrant appointed by Cassander (295 B.C.). Taking the city by storm, he relieved the wants of the poor by a distribution of grain—the only revenge he seems to have inflicted for their bad conduct towards him. The fortification of the Piræus, Munychia, and the Museum Hill, however, showed his resolve to hold the city now with a stronger grasp. His invasion of the Peloponnesus was brought to a sudden end by news from Macedonia, where a disputed succession, consequent on the death of Cassander afforded him an opportunity of interfering.

In a short time he made himself master of Macedonia, the throne of which he held for seven years (294-287). Dethroned then by Pyrrhus, who also yielded in seven months to Lysimachus, he sank through a series of disasters, until death ended his career in a Syrian dungeon, the captive of Seleucus (283 B.C.)

CHAPTER IV.

THE ACHÆAN LEAGUE.

Gauls at Delphi. Pyrrhus. Aratus. | Agis and Cleomenes. Cleomenean War. Battle of Sellasia. | Social War. Death of Aratus.

UNDER a returned exile named Demochares, who became ruler after a revolution, by which the Macedonians were expelled, Athens enjoyed a brief glimpse of peace and prosperity.

A new foe now began to menace Grecian freedom in the shape of wild Celts, who came swooping like birds of prey from the mountains, scenting the plunder of the temple at Delphi. Avoiding, by the very hill-path taken by the Persian host, a Grecian army posted at Thermopylæ, Brennus led his barbarians into the heart of Greece, and approached the shrine. But the earth began to shake—it thundered and lightened—rocks, torn from the cliff, all sheeted with sudden snow and ice, crushed the audacious savages, upon whom the Greeks fell on every side. Next night in a panic they turned their blows on one another; and but few escaped from Greece, which had proved to them a land of terror and of death.

279 B.C.

We shall hear of Pyrrhus of Epirus in Roman history. On his return from his Italian expedition, he wrested the sceptre of Macedonia from Antigonus Gonatas, but held it for only two years (274–72). He met with a sturdy resistance at Sparta, where the resolution of the citizens impeded his attack by digging a deep trench and ranging waggons in a barricade at each end. Generous aid from their ancient foe, the Messenians, and the approach of reinforcements from Antigonus, saved the city. Pyrrhus then turned away to Argos, where the army of Antigonus occupied the heights. A gate being opened to him, Pyrrhus got within the walls; but, as the elephants, cumbered with their towers, were trying to struggle through the narrow entrance, one of them was killed, and its huge body blocked the way. In the confusion and fighting that ensued, a tile, flung from a housetop by a woman, stunned Pyrrhus, and an enemy then cut off his head (272 B.C.).

Antigonus Gonatas, being restored, then reigned in Macedon without interruption until 239 B.C. Greece was meanwhile overrun with brigands and homeless exiles, who had no resource but plunder.

Yet the sun of Grecian glory, though verging to a swift descent, was not quite set. The names of Aratus, Cleomenes, and Philopœmen shed some lustre on the closing pages of a splendid story.

Born in 271, Aratus at the age of seven found himself fatherless and an exile from his native town of Sicyon. At Argos, where he lived in youth, his name was foremost in the wrestling-ring and all scenes of athletic sport. He had little trouble in persuading a band of exiles to aid him in surprising Sicyon. The dogs of a certain gardener living by the wall, where they intended to clamber up, caused them most dread; and some of them, in the guise of travellers, sought a lodging in this man's house, for the purpose of keeping the animals quiet. But in this they did not succeed; and the midnight sky resounded with the howling of many
dogs. But in spite of passing sentinels, baying
251 dogs, crowing cocks, and breaking day, Aratus and
B.C. his friends scaled the wall and seized the guard-
house. A summons from the theatre called forth the citizens at sunrise to receive liberty. The tyrant fled by a subterranean passage; and Sicyon was free.

Aratus at once joined the Achæan League. This confederacy, which had been in existence since 280, owed its origin to the dread entertained of Macedonian ascendency by four towns of Achaia—Dyme, Patræ, Tritæa, and Pharæ. It was a democratic association, and held its synods twice a year at Ægion, under the presidency of a magistrate called *Strategus*. The great object of the League, which gradually attracted many towns, was to set the Peloponnesus free But it was not until Aratus secured for it the adhesion of Sicyon that the confederacy assumed great prominence in Grecian politics.

There was another, but less respectable, League, formed by the mountaineers of Ætolia for the selfish purpose of their own aggrandizement. It held its annual meeting at Thermon.

Aratus was made Strategus of the Achæan League in 245 B.C.; and to this office he was recalled seventeen times. After a campaign in Locris and Calydonia he made a movement to expel Antigonus from Corinth. By night he forced his way into the city; and, appearing in the morning on the stage of the theatre in full armour, he gave the keys of the gate to the citizens amid thunders of applause. This resulted in the adhesion of Corinth to the Achæan League. Megara, Epidaurus, Troezen, even Argos followed the example of Corinth; so that under the skilful direction of Aratus the League had now assumed the proportions of "a powerful confederation, including the whole northern coast of Peloponnesus, from the promontory of Araxas to Scyllæum, with the lands of Corinth and Megara, and the greater part of Arcadia."

243 B.C.

During the growth of the League a Spartan King named Agis had been forming in his mind the glorious but impossible dream of restoring corrupted Sparta to the ancient strength and virtue she had enjoyed under the legislation of Lycurgus. His colleague Leonidas, unworthy wearer of a glorious name, was opposed to his scheme of reform. Agis was murdered; and his widow was obliged to marry Cleomenes the son of Leonidas. This lady so wrought upon her devoted young husband that he longed for the power to perfect the plan of reform shaped out by Agis. But the Ephors at that time held the real authority in Sparta, the King being a mere puppet in their hands. Cleomenes therefore sought to kindle a war, by which the way might be cleared for the accomplishment of his design.

The main object of the Achæan League being the union of all the Peloponnesian states into one compact body, it is little wonder that Sparta, aiming at a similar end, should come into collision with that confederacy. Besides Lacedæmon, Elis and some towns of Arcadia were the only parts of the peninsula that had not joined the Achæan League. Aratus entered Ar-

226 B.C.

cadia with an army; and the Ephors sent Cleomenes to meet him. During the first campaign Aratus would not fight, even though he commanded twenty thousand men in opposition to only five thousand Spartans. Next year a defeat at Mount Lyceum obliged Aratus to retreat; but he turned the loss into a gain by seizing Mantinea and forcing it to join the League. But Cleomenes then won a signal advantage at Megalopolis. Lydiades the prince of that city, by a rash charge into a place tangling with vines and broken with ditches, lost both the battle and his life. Cleomenes defeated the whole Achæan army.

Advancing to Sparta with his mercenaries, Cleomenes sent some youths to slay the Ephors as they sat at supper. He then divided all the land; and the black broth was once more served to the Spartan men at their common dining-tables.

Cleomenes resumed his career of victory. He retook Mantinea. He defeated the Achæans at Dyme. Invading Achaia, he conquered Pellene—then surprised Argos, and laid siege to the citadel of Corinth.

Aratus, refusing the office of *Strategus*, called in the aid of Antigonus Doson, King of Macedonia, who acceded for the sake of the promised reward—the Acro-
224 B.C. Corinthus. Cleomenes, digging a ditch across the Isthmus, defended it for a time, until obliged to abandon his position owing to the march of Aratus to Argos, then in the throes of a revolt. Antigonus, entering the Peloponnesus, was elected commander of the Achæan army. Next year witnessed successes on both sides; but the decisive battle of Sellasia ruined the hopes of Cleomenes in 222 B.C.

The Spartan King with twenty thousand men occupied the pass of Sellasia on the road to Argos. Two steep hills formed the sides of the defile, and Cleomenes had
222 B.C. strengthened a position naturally strong with a rampart and ditch. After a hot cavalry battle, in which Philopœmen, a young officer of Megalopolis, greatly distinguished himself, the phalanxes closed with a terrific shock, the Spartans at first gaining some advantage, but the weight of the Macedonian armour at last telling

victoriously on the opposing mass. Cleomenes, fleeing from the field, got away in a ship to Egypt, where after a wild attempt to excite a revolution in Alexandria he fell upon his sword and died (220 B.C.).

In the same year the Social War between the Achæan and Ætolian Leagues broke out. The Ætolians, invading the Peloponnesus, began to ravage Messenia, whose inhabitants called in the aid of the Achæan army. Aratus, the Strategus, led a force into the field; but was defeated in Arcadia by the Ætolians, who continued their ravages as they went northward to the Isthmus on their way home.

Philip V., the successor of Antigonus on the throne of Macedon, attended an Achæan congress at Corinth, at which a decree was passed against the Ætolians.

In 219 B.C. Philip took the town of Ambracia, and by way of Acarnania carried fire and sword into Ætolia. The danger of his own kingdom obliged him to abandon his enterprise for a time. The next winter saw him in the Peloponnesus, wading through mountain-snow, to invade Elis. The capture of many towns rewarded his daring. He then retired to Argos.

Philip soon afterwards caused a rival of Aratus to be elected to the post of Strategus. The choice was unlucky; but Philip's energy made up for the deficiency of the feeble Achæan. Thermon, the capital of Ætolia, was sacked. The Peloponnesus was wasted to its southern capes. The victory of Hannibal at Lake Trasimene however excited the ambition of Philip, who began to revolve in his mind a war with Rome. To engage in this unhindered was his primary object in concluding the peace of 217, which left all parties as they were.

An estrangement had for some time been growing up between Philip and Aratus; and at last, according to the common account, a slow poison was administered to the old soldier by order of the King of Macedon (213 B.C.).

CHAPTER V.

ROMANS ON THE SCENE.

First Macedonian War.
Philopœmen.
Cynoscephalæ.
The Syrian War.
Degradation of Sparta.
Battle of Pydna.
Fall of Corinth.

THE conclusion of a treaty between Philip of Macedon and the victorious Hannibal in 215 B.C. was a primary cause of Roman interference in the affairs of Greece. Demetrius of Pharos, once prince of Illyria, was Philip's chief adviser at this time.

The First Macedonian War (215–205) progressed feebly. A squadron of Roman ships, stationed at Tarentum, watched lest Philip might attempt to invade Italy. But in 211 the Roman general made alliance with the Ætolian League on terms pleasant to those plunderers. This obliged Philip to bestir himself. The Achæan League was on his side, while the Lacedæmonians were the principal adherents of the Romans and Ætolians. The Romans did not enter with any zeal into a war on Grecian soil, for their great object was to keep Philip so employed in Greece that he should not be able to aid Hannibal. Their general therefore did little more than take Ægina, and excite hostilities against the Macedonian. Peace was made in 205 B.C.

The new leader of the Achæan League was Philopœmen of Megalopolis, a man devoted to the art of war, and worthily styled "The last of the Greeks." His valour had mainly contributed to the victory of Sellasia; and we shall see in a little how he dealt with Sparta, the constant foe of the League he represented.

Philip broke the peace with Rome by sending men to assist Hannibal at the battle of Zama. He also joined Antiochus of Syria in an attempt to rob the young Egyptian King of his dominions; and ravaged Attica with great cruelty. The Romans, now free from the troubles of a Punic War, thought it right to check him in his career. The Second Macedonian War then began, 200 B.C.

Reluctantly the Roman people plunged into a new war; but their rulers forced the point. After taking Abydos in the north, Philip came southwards and wasted the environs of Athens, to the great disgust of his Achæan allies. Galba the Roman general, and his successor did little to maintain the reputation of the Roman sword; but, when Flamininus came upon the scene, there was a decided change. Philip now met his match, and more. During his first campaign he forced Philip to withdraw from Thessaly into Macedonia; and by keeping a Roman fleet anchored at one of the ports of Corinth gained such an ascendency that the Achæan League voted for alliance with Rome, contrary to the wish of Philopœmen, who would rather have remained neutral in the war.

After a conference at Thermopylæ Philip sent an envoy to Rome. The Senate demanded to know whether he was prepared to evacuate Demetrias, Chalcis, and Corinth, three fortresses which he was wont to call "the Fetters of Greece." The envoy could give no definite answer, and was accordingly ordered to leave Rome.

The Proconsul Flamininus soon afterwards gained over Thebes and Sparta. The rivals then advanced to meet each other in Thessaly, the Romans being rendered somewhat stronger by the Ætolian cavalry. After some manœuvres the armies encamped one day, unwittingly, on opposite sides of a hilly ridge called Cynoscephalæ. In the drenching mist of the morning Philip sent some light troops to the summit for the purpose of keeping watch; while at the same time a detachment of Romans were climbing the opposite slope. Coming into collision on the brow of the hill, the two bands fought till the Romans were driven down to their outposts, who turned the scale and drove the Macedonians up the hill again. So the battle wavered up and down the slope for a time. Philip, against his own convictions, to please his officers, led a double phalanx to attack the legions, though the ground was broken. The weight of one armed mass,

197 B.C.

bristling with spearheads, that came pouring down the hill, broke the Roman line; but Flamininus had meanwhile sent his elephants up the hill to assail the other portion of the phalanx, which had been all disordered by the uneven ground. The ruin of this body of men cost Philip the battle; and he fled.

A year later, amid deep silence, succeeded by a wild cry of joy, the victorious Roman in the Corinthian amphitheatre proclaimed THAT GREECE WAS FREE; and had some difficulty in escaping suffocation from the heaps of garlands flung upon his head (196 B.C.).

Philopœmen, who some time earlier had conquered a Spartan tyrant at Mantinea, and whose restless spirit sought action in the wars of Crete, when there was an interval of peace at home, now made war upon Nabis the cruel tyrant of Sparta, who, as the enemy of the Achæan League, had formed an alliance with the Ætolians. Nabis was murdered at a review by the leader of the Ætolians, whose aim was to seize Sparta. But the Spartans rose; and, when Philopœmen advanced to the city, they yielded to his wish, and joined the Achæan League, which thus overspread the whole Peloponnesus, except Elis.

A storm was now gathering between Rome and Syria, over which Antiochus ruled. In spite of a stern warning from Flamininus Antiochus ventured to set foot on Europe, having already seized the Greek cities of Asia Minor. His design was much encouraged by Hannibal, who, overcome by political intrigues, had fled from Carthage to Ephesus. Hannibal's advice to the Syrian was to set apart under himself ten thousand men for the invasion of Italy, and go in person across to Greece, whither he had been invited by the Ætolians. Landing at Demetrias, and disregarding Hannibal's other advice, the Syrian monarch did little more during the year 192 than take a few towns in Thessaly, and fall back on Chalcis in Eubœa to celebrate his marriage.

Next year Antiochus met the Roman Consul in the pass of Thermopylæ, and was defeated there, exactly as the heroic Leonidas had been defeated. The mountain path was committed to the Ætolians; but they neglected it for the plunder of a town, so that Flaccus and Cato crossed the ridge with ease and attacked the Syrians in the rear. Porcius Cato, one of the lieutenants, by whom the victory was gained, carried the news to Rome *via* Tarentum.

Then by order of Flamininus Elis and Messenia joined the Achæan League, which at last extended over all the Peloponnesus.

The two Scipios, Africanus and his brother, proceeded to Greece in 190 B.C., resolved to follow Antiochus into Asia. Philip of Macedon smoothed their way to the Hellespont. Hannibal, acting in command of a Phœnician fleet, was defeated. Antiochus had mustered a vast Oriental army, in which elephants and dromedaries abounded. With this he took post at Magnesia under Mount Sipylus, whither the elder Scipio followed him. It was not until he saw that he could not help himself that the Syrian drew out his men. In spite of his vast army he was totally defeated with immense loss; and, when he had fled into a safe place, he begged humbly for peace. The terms were hard. Surrendering all his possessions north of Taurus, and paying a large sum in war-costs and tribute, he was ordered to interfere in no European affairs, and to give up Hannibal to the Romans.

The Spartans came into collision with the Achæans in 189 B.C. Some of them, indignant at being cut off from the sea by the arrangements of Flamininus, went one night and seized the sea-port Las, from which however the people soon expelled them. A complaint was lodged against the perpetrators of this violence; and the Achæans required Sparta to surrender the guilty persons. In a rage the Spartans killed some of the Achæan faction, renounced the League, and offered the protection of their city to the Roman Consul. When Philopœmen came in spring with an army to enforce his demand that the violators of the treaty should be given up, these persons, to the number of eighty, went, after receiving a pledge of security, to the Achæan camp. Some of them were stoned at once by a mob: the rest, after a mock trial, were executed. And Philopœmen then inflicted upon Sparta a disgraceful doom, obliging the citizens to raze their walls and to abandon the system of Lycurgus.

The revolt of Messenia in 183 called Philopœmen from a fevered bed to the saddle. Seventy years had not quenched his martial fire. Having routed the rebels, he was retreating over rough ground, when his horse threw him, and he was taken prisoner. The people of Messenia were so full of admiring pity for the gallant old warrior that his captors resolved on sudden and extreme measures. He was put into a pit called the Treasury, the mouth of which was covered with a ponderous slab of stone; and then at midnight he was roused from the rest he was taking, wrapped in his cloak, to drink a cup of poison. His body was rescued by the Leaguers; and a flower-draped urn, containing his ashes, was borne with reverential sorrow to the place of his birth, where the Messenian prisoners were stoned at his tomb.

The Third Macedonian War with Rome began in 171 B.C., after Perseus, the son and successor of Philip, had spent many years in preparation. It lingered for some campaigns, during which fortune rather favoured the Macedonian arms. But Æmilius Paullus, the son-in-law of Scipio, becoming Consul, crossed to the scene of war. The decisive engagement, which overturned for ever the throne of Macedon, took place on the plain of Pydna. A runaway horse from the Roman lines being seized by some Thracian

168 B.C.

sentinels, a contest ensued, which attracted many soldiers from both sides. This skirmish grew into a general engagement. Paullus, though he wisely kept the thought concealed, looked with a strange fear on the phalanx, serried with points. The onset at first justified his fear, for the weight of the phalanx drove back the legions. But, when the battle swayed towards hilly ground, the *sarissa* proved a burden, and the Macedonian ranks fell to pieces. The Romans penetrated the gaps of the line, and signally defeated the army.

Thus ended the Macedonian monarchy. Perseus surrendered to the Romans at Samothrace, and spent his life as their pensioner in Italy.

The Romans then carried one thousand of the chief Achæans as hostages to Rome. The most famous of the number was Polybius the historian. After sixteen years of suffering three hundred survivors were sent back to Greece.

The last effort of the League was a frantic and hopeless war with Rome, fomented by Critolaus the Strategus. Before the Consul Mummius arrived at the scene of action, Metellus, the Roman governor of Macedonia, had twice defeated Critolaus, who lost his life, probably by drowning in a marsh, after the second action. His successor Diæus concentrated the forces of the League at Corinth. Emboldened by a slight success over some outposts, he challenged the Roman army, now under the command of Mummius, to battle at Leucopetra near Corinth. The Achæan cavalry were broken at once; and the infantry laid down their lives in vain. The battle was irretrievably lost, and with it sank the hopes of Greece.

146 B.C.

Mummius, a few days later, set fire to Corinth. Diæus slew his wife and then poisoned himself. Even the name of Greece suffered eclipse, for as a Roman province it was called Achaia.

Just sixty years later, Athens, the centre of Grecian learning and taste, suffered the horrors of plunder and massacre at the hands of pitiless Sulla, because the rabble of the city had declared in favour of Mithridates, then at war with Rome.

GREAT NAMES OF GRECIAN LITERATURE, &c.

THIRD PERIOD.

ÆSCHINES, Athenian orator—born 389 B.C.—the great rival of Demosthenes—defeated in the Case of the Crown—retired to Rhodes and Samos—died 314 B.C.

DEMOSTHENES, Athenian orator—born about 385 B.C.—poisoned himself at Calaurea 322 B.C. (see pp. 113-14)—most famous among his *Orations* are the *Philippics* and the *Speech on the Crown* (*Peri Stephanou*).

PRAXITELES, great sculptor of Athens—flourished about 364 B.C.—chief work his *Aphrodite* or Venus.

SCOPAS of Paros (flourished 395-350 B.C.), was also a great sculptor and architect—chief work *Children of Niobe Destroyed.*

ARISTOTLE, Macedonian philosopher—born 384 B.C. at Stagira—pupil of Plato at Athens—tutor of Alexander the Great—taught in the Lyceum at Athens, walking up and down—hence founder of the Peripatetic School—wrote on nearly every subject—aided by Alexander in his *History of Animals*—died 322 B.C. at Chalcis in Eubœa.

APELLES, Grecian painter—contemporary of Alexander the Great—chief works, *Alexander* as a god, and *Venus* rising from the sea—born probably at Colophon in Ionia.

LYSIPPUS was the chief contemporary sculptor.

ZENO, Stoic philosopher—born about 362 B.C. at Citium in Cyprus—wrecked in the Piræus—settled in Athens—taught in a porch (*Stoa*), hence his disciples were called Stoics—died probably about 264 B.C.

EPICURUS, philosopher—born at Samos 342 B.C.—lived chiefly at Athens, where he founded the Epicurean School—taught that happiness, resulting from peace of mind and a virtuous life, was the *Summum bonum*—died 270 B.C.

MENANDER, writer of the New Comedy—born at Athens 342 B.C.—drowned in the Piræus, while bathing, 291 B.C.—Terence translated largely from his comedies, which have been lost.

PHILEMON was another writer of the New Comedy.

ENCLID, mathematician—lived at Alexandria (323-283 B.C.)—told Ptolemy I. there was no "royal road" to the knowledge of geometry—best known work called *The Elements.*

THEOCRITUS, Sicilian pastoral poet—born at Syracuse—lived under Ptolemy Soter and Ptolemy Philadelphus at Alexandria, then under Hiero II. in Sicily—author of *Idyls.* BION of Smyrna, and MOSCHUS of Syracuse also cultivated Bucolic poetry.

ARCHIMEDES, celebrated mathematician—born at Syracuse 287 B.C.—friend of Hiero—his engines aided in the defence of Syracuse against Marcellus—killed by a Roman soldier 212 B.C.

ARISTARCHUS, celebrated critic—native of Samothrace—flourished about 156 B.C.—taught grammar at Alexandria—starved himself to death in Cyprus—chief work an *Edition of the Homeric Poems.*

POLYBIUS, historian—born about 204 B.C. at Megalopolis in Arcadia—went to Italy as an Achæan hostage in 168 B.C.—travelled much after the fall of Corinth—we possess only five entire books of his *History*, which extended from 220 B.C. to 146 B.C.

APOLLODORUS, grammarian and mythologist—flourished at Athens about 140 B.C.—author of *Bibliotheca*, an account of the Greek mythology.

GREAT NAMES OF GRECIAN LITERATURE UNDER THE ROMANS.

DIONYSIUS, of Halicarnassus—lived under Augustus at Rome—chief work *History of Rome* down to 264 B.C.—but greater as a literary critic—died B.C. 7.

DIODORUS SICULUS, historian—born at Agyrium in Sicily—contemporary of Julius Cæsar and Augustus—author of *Bibliotheca Historica*, ending with the opening of Cæsar's Gallic wars, (fifteen books preserved entire out of forty)—not reliable.

STRABO, native of Amasia in Pontus—born about 54 B.C.—continued the History of Polybius, but more celebrated for his *Geography*—died about 24 A.D.

PLUTARCH, biographer—born at Chæronea in Bœotia about the reign of Claudius—lectured at Rome—was a magistrate at Chæronea—great work, *Parallel Lives* of Greeks and Romans—author also of *Moralia*, or ethical discourses.

EPICTETUS, Stoic philosopher of Hierapolis in Phrygia—his pupil, Arrian, compiled the *Enchiridion* from his lectures—lived at Rome, from which Domitian expelled him.

GALEN, celebrated physician—born at Pergamum A.D. 130—practised at Rome ultimately—died about 200 A.D.—author of many *Treatises.*

ARRIAN, a Greek historian—born about 90 A.D. at Nicomedia in Bithynia—prefect of Cappadocia in 136, consul in 146—chief work, *History of the Expedition of Alexander the Great*—died in the reign of Aurelius.

DION CASSIUS, historian—born 155 A.D. at Nicæa in Bithynia—son of a Roman senator—chief work, *History of Rome* (from landing of Æneas to 229 A.D.)—of 80 books we have 18—remarkable for his judgment and research.

APPIAN, an historian—native of Alexandria—flourished under Trajan, Hadrian, and Antoninus Pius—author of a *Roman History*, which is a compilation.

LUCIAN, Greek satirist—born at Samosata in Syria—flourished under Aurelius—a procurator in Egypt—chief work, the *Dialogues*.

PAUSANIAS, geographer—born probably in Lydia—lived in the reigns of Antoninus and Aurelius—author of *Periegesis*, an Itinerary of Greece, descriptive of that land.

ÆLIAN, a writer on Natural History—born at Præneste in the third century—works, *Varia Historia* and *De Animalium Natura* (on the Nature of Animals).

ATHENÆUS, of Naucratis in Egypt—lived about 230 A.D.—went to Rome—author of *Deipnosophistae* (*the Banquet of the Learned*), *a book of Table-talk and Anecdote.*

HERODIAN, compiler—*Roman History* (180-238 A.D.)—native of Alexandria—flourished about 247 A.D.

GRECIAN CHRONOLOGY.

	B.C.
Fall of Troy, ...	1184
The Æolian Migration, ...	1124
The Dorian Migration, ...	1104
Codrus the Athenian martyr-king slain, ...	1068
Lycurgus the Spartan legislator, ...	884
Beginning of the *Olympiads*	776
The First Messenian War, ...	743–723
The Second Messenian War, ...	685–668
Draco's blood-stained Laws at Athens, ...	624
Cylon's plot endangers Athens, ...	612

SIXTH CENTURY, B.C.

Solon chosen Archon at Athens, ...	594
Pisistratus makes himself Tyrant of Athens, ...	560
His death and accession of his three sons, ...	527
The Pisistratids expelled, ...	510
The Ionian Greeks revolt from Persia, ...	500

FIFTH CENTURY, B.C.

THE FIRST PERSIAN WAR.

A Persian army under Mardonius invades Greece, ...	492
Battle of Marathon, ...	490

THE SECOND PERSIAN WAR.

Invasion of Xerxes, ...	480
Battle of Thermopylæ, ...	—
Battle of Artemisium, ...	—
Battle of Salamis, ...	—
Battles of Platæa and Mycale, ...	479

Third Messenian War, ... 464–455
Thirty Years' Truce between Sparta and Athens, ... 445
Splendour of Athens under Pericles, ... 445–429

THE PELOPONNESIAN WAR.

Peloponnesian War begins, ... 432
Night march of Thebans upon Platæa, ... 431
Death of Pericles, ... 429
Revolt of Lesbos from Athens, ... 428
Platæa surrenders to Sparta, ... 427
Sphacteria taken by Cleon, the tanner, ... 425
Battle of Delium, ... 424
Athenians defeated at Amphipolis—Brasidas and Cleon killed, 422
The Peace of Nicias (for fifty years), ... 421
The attack on Orchomenus breaks the peace, ... 421
First Battle of Mantinea, ... 418
Expedition of Athenians to Sicily, ... 415
Siege of Syracuse begins, ... —
Destruction of the Athenian army, ... 413
Victory of Alcibiades at Cyzicus, ... 410
Return of Alcibiades to Athens, ... 407
Naval victory of the Athenians at Arginusæ, ... 406
Decisive victory of Lysander at Ægos-potami, ... 405
Surrender of Athens and end of the war, ... 404

The Thirty Tyrants deposed by Thrasybulus, ... 403
Cyrus sets out from Sardis with the Ten Thousand, ... 401
Battle of Cunaxa, ... 400

FOURTH CENTURY, B.C.

Death of Socrates, ... 399
Agesilaus on the Spartan throne, ... —
Battle of Coronea, ... 394
Conon rebuilds the Athenian walls, ... 393
The Peace of Antalcidas, ... 387

THEBAN WAR.

The Cadmea seized by Phœbidas, ... 382
The Exiles deliver Thebes, ... 379
Battle of Orchomenus, ... 375
Battle of Leuctra, ... 371
Restoration of Ithome by Epaminondas, ... 369
Death of Pelopidas in Thessaly, ... 364
Second or great Battle of Mantinea, and death of Epaminondas, 362

PHILIP OF MACEDON.

Philip ascends the throne of Macedon, ...	359
He takes the city of Amphipolis, ...	358
Social War—between Athens and her Allies	357–55
Sacred or Theban War, ...	357–46
Philomelus seizes Delphi, ...	357
Invasion of Thessaly by Philip, ...	352
Demosthenes delivers the First Philippic, ...	—
Philip takes Olynthus, ...	348
Philip overruns Phocis, ...	346
The Athenians resolve on war with Philip, ...	340
They relieve Perinthus and Byzantium, ...	—
Philip seizes Elatea, ...	339
Battle of Chæronea, ...	338
Murder of Philip at Ægæ, ...	336

ALEXANDER THE GREAT.

Destruction of Thebes by Alexander, ...	335
Alexander crosses the Hellespont, ...	334
Battle of the Granicus, ...	—
Battle of Issus, ...	333
Sieges of Tyre and Gaza, ...	332
Alexandria founded, ...	331
Battle of Gaugamela or Arbela, ...	331
Capture of the Sogdian Rock, ...	328
March to the Punjaub, ...	326
Battle of the Hydaspes, ...	—
Descent of the Indus, ...	325
Death of Alexander at Babylon, ...	323
The Lamian War, ...	323–22
Death of Demosthenes, ...	322
Partition of Triparadisus, ...	—
Cassander's occupation of Athens, ...	318
Second Partition of the Alexandrian Empire, ...	311
Demetrius Poliorcetes takes Athens, ...	307
Reduces Cyprus, ...	306
Is repulsed at Rhodes, ...	305
Return of Demetrius to Athens, ...	303
Battle of Ipsus—Third Partition, ...	301

THIRD CENTURY, B.C.

Demetrius occupies Athens a third time, ...	295
Holds the Macedonian sceptre, ...	294–87

Dies in a Syrian prison, ...	283
The Celts at Delphi, ...	279
Death of Pyrrhus, ...	272
Aratus delivers Sicyon, ...	251
Aratus made Strategus of the Achæan League, ...	245
War between Cleomenes and Aratus, ...	226–22
Aratus asks aid from Antigonus Doson, ...	224
Battle of Sellasia, ...	222
Social War (Achæans against Ætolians), ...	220–17
First Macedonian War with Rome, ...	215–05
Aratus poisoned by Philip, ...	213

SECOND CENTURY, B.C.

Second Macedonian War, ...	200–197
Battle of Cynoscephalæ, ...	197
Greece proclaimed free by Flamininus, ...	196
The Syrian War, ...	192–190
Battle of Magnesia, ...	190
Philopœmen abolishes the laws of Lycurgus, ...	188
Death of Philopœmen, ...	183
Third Macedonian War with Rome, ...	171–68
Battle of Pydna—End of the Macedonian Monarchy, ...	168
Battle of Leucopetra—Burning of Corinth, and close of ancient Grecian history, ...	146

CPSIA information can be obtained
at www.ICGtesting.com
Printed in the USA
LVHW100612210323
742065LV00002B/263